Am I Still
in Love
With You?

Am I Still in Love With You?

Sudhanshu Anand

Srishti
PUBLISHERS & DISTRIBUTORS

SRISHTI PUBLISHERS & DISTRIBUTORS
Registered Office: N-16, C.R. Park
New Delhi – 110 019
Corporate Office: 212A, Peacock Lane
Shahpur Jat, New Delhi – 110 049
editorial@srishtipublishers.com

First published by
Srishti Publishers & Distributors in 2018

Copyright © Sudhanshu Anand, 2018

10 9 8 7 6 5 4 3 2 1

Printed at Repro Knowledgecast Limited, Thane

Dedicated to my mother
and
my grandfather
and
To all those who loved someone
whole-heartedly and lost them early in life.

Acknowledgement

THOSE WHO ARE GOING TO READ THIS NOVEL, thank you for the love, support and trust in my work.

This novel is the reflection of my understanding of life through the people who were with me till now. So thank you for teaching me the lessons of life at every stage.

Shubham Aashu, my friend, my brother, thank you for the support, faith and trust as a friend throughout these years.

My mother Mrs Rita, father Mr Sagar Paswan, brother Amritanshu and my beautiful sister Sweety – you guys are the four strong pillars who have supported me in my ups and downs. You guys are truly an inspiration for me.

To the place and the people of Sitamarhi – this book is a payback to the place where I grew and understood the concepts of being on this earth.

Thank you to my extended family and beloved friends on Facebook and Twitter.

Heartfelt thanks to team Srishti Publishers for believing in me and this piece of art.

Prologue

2ⁿᵈ December 2011
Kota, Rajasthan

"DUDE, WHAT ARE YOUR PLANS AFTER YOUR JEE exam?" Ambika asked holding her cup of tea.

"I don't know babe, AIEEE or some other shit exam," I said and took my cup from the tea guy.

"No, I mean which college do you want to go to?" she asked.

It was a regular meeting for us at I.L. Colony's street. We were sitting at our favourite spot and had just ordered two cups of tea from the tea shop. I looked at her and saw something different, which was strange. She was looking beautiful and serious at the same moment. I put my cup down.

"I don't know, it depends on my results. Moreover, why are you getting serious about this? I will definitely take admission at the place where you will be," I said to make her comfortable, holding her hand in mine.

"Yesterday, I was talking to my dad and he told me that I will be studying in Ludhiana Medical College," she said, concerned.

"Don't worry, I will also take admission in Ludhiana," I said and picked the cup up to take a sip.

"Oh yeah, which college? There is no such college for you there. They all are regional average colleges," she said in anger.

"Ohkk…" I said and was still trying to understand why she was reacting in this way.

"I think we should break-up!" she said suddenly.

There was silence for a minute. For that one minute, suddenly I was able to hear each and every sound from my surroundings. I continued looking into her eyes all that time, but was blank. I opened my mouth and was able to say nothing as I was still in complete shock.

"I don't want you to be in a college which is not good enough for you just because of me. Look, I love you and I want you to be at the place where you belong. I don't want you to compromise with your college just because of me," she continued.

"Listen, we will not meet for a few days and we will see whether we miss each other or not. We will not call each other, and will not try to contact each other in any possible way," she completed in a weepy voice.

"Okay," I said, still trying to make sense of what she had said.

That's it, she leaned forward and kissed me on my lips gently, got up and walked towards her hostel. I still sat on that spot as I saw her slowly getting out of my sight.

I still don't understand why I said okay to her. Maybe I wanted the same. The following week, we didn't meet, call each other or text. So I had much time to think and process everything related with Ambika.

The break-up with Ambika was smooth; there was no drama, no anger, and no tears. Why didn't it happen at that time?

Yes, at that time. The time when I was not having the guts to say that she was the love of my life. I was just fifteen-and-a-half, but that's the way I used to feel then.

As I was not talking to Ambika. I had time and I wanted to fix the story. The story you are going to read. I wanted her to know that I was not cheating on her with anyone. So I approached Shweta, a common friend of ours, on Facebook, and told her that I wanted to talk to her.

Well, Shweta was in the same section as me and Shikha. She agreed to give me her number after some drama, but advised me to call her only when she'd say so. And I will always appreciate her for her help.

The following two conversations on the cell phone were my hardest attempts to make her understand the whole mess created back then. I wanted her to know that my love for her was true and I never thought of cheating on her with anyone, "till we were together".

10ᵗʰ December 2011
Kota, Rajasthan

SHWETA CALLED ME AT HALF PAST SIX IN THE evening. I was lying on my bed and watching *Bigg Boss* on my cell phone in my room in Rose Residency Hostel in Rajeev Gandhi Nagar.

Although I didn't like to be disturbed by anyone when I watched the show, but the moment I saw her name appearing on the screen of my mobile, I immediately took the call.

"Hello," I said.

"Sudhanshu, I talked to her now. You can call her," she said.

"Okay, I am calling her," I said and got out of the bed in sheer excitement.

My room was ten feet by eight feet with a washroom attached to it. I had a bed, a sturdy wooden table with a plastic chair where I used to keep my books, a wardrobe and the luxury of an air conditioner.

I immediately went out of my room, and down the staircase. I used to live on the eighth floor of the hostel. I ran out of the building to recharge my cell phone in the nearest shop.

Since it was evening time, there was a crowd at the shop.

"Munna!" I shouted out really loud.

Munna was the owner of the recharge shop. A typical tall and lean-figured Jaipur guy with the same hair cut that Ajay Devgn sported in the late 1990s.

Everybody turned towards me. I had shouted my lungs out. Munna looked at me and was surprised.

"Yes bhaiya?" he said.

"Munna, recharge my number as soon as possible," I said.

Munna looked at me and understood the urgency. He had my number, so he did it immediately.

"I will give you the money later," I said.

I am not sure whether he heard it or not, but I was almost halfway to my hostel by the time I completed the sentence. I went out to the terrace to talk peacefully, with a good network.

I went to one corner of the terrace and dialled her number, but cut it immediately. I took a deep breath and dialled the number again. This time it rang, and after five rings, she picked up the call.

"Hello," Shikha said.

"Hello," I said.

Honestly, I was very happy to hear her voice after such a long time. I become nervous and was not able to say what I had practiced earlier. I went numb for a few seconds.

"Helloo," she said in irritation.

"Hello. Shikha. How are you?" I said.

"I am good. How are you?" she said after a while. We were talking after a long time.

"I am also good. Where are you right now?" I replied.

"I am in Patna," she said.

"Patna? Ohkay! What are you doing in Patna?" I asked.

"Why do you want to know?" she said softly.

"Because I care about you," I said.

"You care about me? What happened? She left you?" she almost shouted.

"Nobody has left me," I said, maintaining my composure.

"Break-up ho gaya?" she asked in frustration.

"What?" I said.

"Only when *you* get the time, then you call me, right? Why didn't you call earlier?"

"I didn't have your number," I said.

"You could have messaged me on Facebook. Else you should have tried to contact me in any possible way like you have now," she said.

"Believe me, I tried, but was not able to get your number. I was not in contact with anybody, and when Shweta told me that you guys talk, then I asked her for your number," I said.

"Why do you want to talk to me anyway?" she asked.

"I wanted to tell you that I was not wrong. I never cheated on you," I said.

"Then what?" she asked.

I paused for a second as I was not expecting this question from her.

"I don't know. But right now, I just want you to know what happened at that time," I said.

"Then what?" she asked again.

She was making it more difficult for me. But I had made up my mind to tell her everything.

"I told you I don't know. Let me tell you my side of the situation, then you tell me whether I was wrong or right?" I said.

Shikha took a deep breath. She was ready to hear me out.

"I want you to listen carefully. I was not cheating you with Mansi or Amrita or with any other girl in the coaching classes. It was all hyped by Amrita and Kamini Priya. I only wanted to talk to Mansi, but the other girls were not happy. Mansi joined our coaching classes during the 9th standard. She used to be alone and you know me… I talk with everybody. So I asked her about herself one day and we chatted fora while. We started talking almost daily and slowly I almost stopped talking with the other girls.

"All the other girls were jealous of Mansi. But I assure you, that it was harmless chatting. She never asked me about you and never did I tell her. Her sister Aakriti and her friend Kurtika also joined the classes and they started teasing her with my name. It was just for fun. I never asked them to stop it; yes, this was my fault. I didn't want to give them any importance because I didn't care about it. I don't know who told you about this and what they told you. You almost stopped talking to me and I never got the chance to explain.

"The communication gap between us widened, and the relation between us worsened. I wish I could have told you anyway, but, due to the reason you were not talking to me and believing in another person's bullshit, I was upset with you. Yes, this can be my fault that I did not try to tell you my side of the story forcefully. Now you tell me whether I was wrong or right?" I ended my explanation.

"I don't know. I want to believe you, but at the same time, I do not," she said in confusion.

"I want you to believe me. I love you and I never lied," I said.

"I believe you, but what about my situation at that time? Do you know how bad I felt at that time? But why you would care about it! You could have talked to me," she said.

"I told you I was upset with you for not believing me and believing them instead," I said.

"Now what?" she said.

"I just want your forgiveness and want to start fresh. I don't know, just as a stranger maybe, and if you want, we can talk," I said.

There was silence.

"Then what?" she asked.

"As I told you, I don't know. I want to start afresh," I said.

"I don't know. I will think about it," she said.

"Okay, that's what I need," I said.

I didn't want to push too hard, so I hung up. It must have been a lot for her to process as it was over three years since the last time we had chatted.

Although she was not fully satisfied, I was happy that at least I was able to explain myself. Now I was waiting for her to call me as I hoped that she believed me.

Few weeks passed, but she didn't call. So I asked Shweta about it and she told me that she must be checking my patience. So I should wait and then call. I had faith in her and so I agreed to give Shikha as much time as she needed.

It was the month of February now, and within a week, I was leaving Kota as my course at Vibrant Institute was completed. So I was looking for the right moment and right attitude to call her again and find out what she thought now.

10th February 2012
Kota, Rajasthan

MY FRIEND SHUBHAM SINHA (ONE OF MY FEW friends in Kota) and I were getting ready to have dinner. We decided to go to Rajdarbar Hotel in Vigyan Nagar. I went to his room which was opposite my room to get a deodorant. Out of nowhere, suddenly I had the urge to call her again. So I did.

"Hello, how are you?"

"Hello. I am good," she said.

"What have you decided?" I asked.

"About what?" she said.

"I mean, about whether I was right or wrong?"

"See, I forgive you, but I can't forgive the pain I have been through," she said.

"I know, but now I have explained everything; it was not me and it wasn't you. It was the time that we didn't handle well. See, I just want to start afresh to have a good memory of our relationship," I said.

I heard some girls laughing behind.

"Who is laughing?"

"Oh, they are my friends," she said.

"Are they listening to me?" I asked with suspicion.

"No," she said.

"Okay, listen, I have to go. I will call you later," I said.

She had put her phone's speaker on and she and her friend were listening to every statement. I got pissed off. Also, I was not happy that she didn't try to call me in these two months.

After this call, she didn't call me again and neither did I. Well, this was not the last conversation between us. We had chatted after that, but on Facebook. First you should know the whole story, then you'll have an idea what really happened back then.

8ᵗʰ July 2006
Sitamarhi

THE LUNCH BELL RANG AS SAMEER, MY BEST
friend, and I went to the washroom. We, along with other
classmates, were enjoying disturbing each other while peeing.
Then Siddharth, a good friend, came with the saddest news for
us.

"Hey Anand (my pet name), Sumedha..." he said.

Well, Siddharth, Sameer and I were best friends who used
to eat, sleep and pee together. I mean, we were not just friends;
we were brothers who used to go everywhere together. We were
in the same age group, in the same class and used to sit together
in class. Many teachers in our school used to say that our match
had been made by god himself in heaven. Siddharth had broad
shoulders and probably was the most attractive amongst us.

I looked back towards him, still peeing.

"What happened?" I said.

"She loves some other guy who is senior to us," he said.

I immediately stopped peeing and zipped up. I didn't wash my hands and held his collar.

"What? How? What happened?"

"Some guy told me that she had proposed to a senior guy," he said and started crying.

Although it was a great shock to me, I held back myself and stayed calm. Sumedha was a girl in our batch, though in another section. Siddharth and I were among the hundreds in our batch who loved her. I would take a moment to say that she was one of the prettiest girls I had seen in my life.

The lunch period was over. Siddharth and I returned to class.

I was sad and sat quietly. I heard someone calling my name; I looked in that direction and saw a girl gesturing and asking for a pencil. It was Shikha, another classmate. Although I had just one pencil, I immediately gave my pencil to her.

The very next day, the same girl was looking at me. She asked me for a pencil again. I gave my pencil to her again.

The next day in the English class, although I had my English book with me, I asked her to give her English book to me.

Although we had been in the same class together, she looked different that day. She was not like any other school girl. She was serious and had short hair reaching her shoulders. She had a great smile with dimples on both cheeks. Those were a few things I noticed about her and felt happy to have some kind of connection with her.

The same night, I had a bad dream where I saw Sumedha with her boyfriend, though I didn't know who the guy was.

Strangely enough, the girl from my class came in my dream with that beautiful smile and big eyes as well. I got up in the morning and remembered the whole dream.

I was rushing to get ready for the class in the morning and was thinking about the dream. I wanted to reach school as soon as possible. I used to ride a bicycle as I lived only five kilometres away. I thought about her all the way to school.

I arrived at school and parked my bicycle at the parking space and rushed to class. As I entered the class, I saw that she was talking to her friends. She saw me and smiled and I just looked at her with a straight face and didn't know how to react. She looked beautiful. I mean, all those years she was in the same class, but I never looked at her or noticed her. And now, suddenly, I was starting to develop feelings for her.

I really wanted her to ask me for a pen or pencil or a book, so that this little adventure could continue. She soon asked me for my Sanskrit book and I felt relaxed.

This give and take was now becoming regular and I also had developed this habit of asking her for help, and she was always happy to do so. One day, during lunch, she came to my bench to discuss the syllabus of the upcoming unit test. It was our first one to one talk.

"Hi," she said and tucked her hair behind her ear.

"Hi," I said and stood up.

"Oh my god, did you listen to the syllabus sir had given just now?" she said with her eyes wide open.

I remained silent for a few seconds. I had become conscious because every other student in the class was watching us.

"No. I mean yes," I said with the manliest voice I could produce at that moment.

"Don't you think it's too much?" she asked.

"Yeah, it's too much," I said and smiled.

"You must have started the preparation for the exam a few days ago," she said.

"Nah," I said as though I had no interest in studying.

"Then, when will you start?"

Although I was not serious about it, but the way she said with her eyes wide open and with concern on her face, it made me wonder whether what I was doing was right or wrong.

I used to, in fact, be among the toppers in the class till seventh standard, but I had not performed well in the exams of eighth standard. There was a reason behind it. It was the time when I was going nuts and had started to behave like a rouge teenager.

"I will start very soon," I said with serious face.

Her concern made her more likable. During the entire discussion, it never appeared to me that this was the first time we were talking in person. We were so lost in the discussion that it never occurred to us that we had to have lunch.

You know, we boys are addicted to some kind of smell, and jeez, she smelled amazing.

The following week, we continued our lunch meetings. Soon it changed to morning meetings, lunch meetings and any other time we could get to spend together.

The Closeness

ONE DAY DURING LUNCH WE WERE TALKING AND she took out one large polythene bag with lots of paper currency in it. She took one out of it.

"You know, this is one of the few things which are very close to me," she said.

I looked at her with a question mark on my face.

"Well, my father is a traveller. He has travelled all around the world and he always brought me the currencies of those countries as a memoir. I like collecting them," she said vey proudly.

She showed me each one, and meanwhile, I was thinking that the only foreign country I had been to was Nepal. And I thought that her father must be an international thief, otherwise it was not possible for any middle class man to travel to so many countries.

She again took an album out of the packet. There were pictures of a lady with Bollywood actors Amrish Puri, Om Puri, Gul Panag and many more.

"She is my mother," she said pointing at the lady who was in all the pictures.

"She is beautiful. What does she do?" I asked.

"She is a designer," she said proudly.

"Great," I said with subdued excitement.

She looked at me and perhaps wanted to know about my subdued reaction on her 'precious' belongings.

"You never told me about your family," she said.

"I will tell you later, when time will come."

She looked right into my eyes and wanted to understand why I had told her this, but then took another photo in her hand and changed the topic.

It was the month of August now, the month of the Rakhi festival. We boys were aware of it and used to avoid coming to school. Although our school remained closed on this day, the girls of our school were clever. It was their only chance to take revenge on those *aashiqs.* So they used to bring many rakhis during the days close to the festival and would tie them on to anyone they'd get hold of; it used to be the last day of *aashiqui* with that girl.

I had arrived in school early on this day. I entered in the class and I saw Shikha, Amit, Sameer, Keshu, and other girls of our class standing together. They were laughing, shouting and making a huge racket.

I saw that and went directly to my bench and put my bag on the bench.

"Sudhanshu, come here!" Sameer shouted from there.

I stood up and went to the girl's row. I was calm and had no idea why he was calling me.

"Yes," I said.

"Now tie one on him also," he told Shikha.

I didn't say any word and stood there silently.

"No, I will not, because he is my friend," she said boldly.

I can't tell you how good I felt at that moment. It changed everything. I was not just a guy from her class, but a guy who was a friend whom she didn't want to convert into a brother.

This incident brought us closer to each other, not just in ours, but in the eyes of other students as well.

Now the role of two kaminas enters the story. They were Shlok and Archit, our classmates. Shlok was the guy who used to sit with me on the same bench. We all used to call him 'Neta' and he used to take politics quite seriously. He used to represent our class on each 'political' stage. Archit, on the other hand, was a wannabe neta and shadow of Shlok. Both of them were opposites, but were always seen together.

I don't know how they got the news of her calling me a friend. The very next day, I was returning home from school on my bicycle. They also used to come to school on bicycles.

I was riding my bicycle slowly through the service road and they came from behind and joined me.

"How are you Sudhanshu?" Archit asked.

"I am good. How come you're coming this way?" I said.

"Yeah! Actually we have some work at Shankar Chowk related to the committee."

I looked at him and ignored him as I knew he would never say the exact truth. Shlok, who was saying nothing till now and was behind us, came forward in the same line in which I and Archit were riding our bicycle.

"Sudhanshu, it's not right," he said.

"What have I done wrong, yaar?" I asked as I had no idea what he was talking about.

"You didn't tell me what Shikha told you the other day," he said.

I didn't want them to know about it so I tried to divert his mind.

"Oh that, arrey… she wanted to tie a rakhi on your hand," I said.

I knew it would ignite his anger and he would change the topic.

"No, not that. What she said about you," he said with calmness, not irritated by my words.

I saw his face and was surprised as he showed no change of facial expression.

"She said you were a friend," Archit said and smiled.

Now it was the time to come out and accept it as they already knew about it.

"Oh that! Yeah, she is a very nice girl," I said.

"Nice girl. Hmm… what do you mean?" Shlok said.

"Arrey… I mean she is a good friend only," I said.

"Bhai, she never calls other guys a friend. Why did she say that about you?" Shlok said.

"What do you mean?" I asked.

"Bhai, I think she likes you," he said.

There are a few things in a boy's life which they understand more when some other guy explains it. And the matter of love also falls in this category.

"What are you talking about?" I said.

"You must have noticed the way she looks at you, she cares for you and whenever you are not present in class, she appears to be distracted and becomes sad and always asks me the reason of your absence," he said.

All his words were making sense to me.

"I think you should propose to her," he continued.

"Arrey… no bhai, it will change everything. What if she says no?" I said knowing the gravity of the thought.

"She will not. She herself has admitted that you are his friend!" he said.

Although I wanted to do that, honestly, I was scared to propose to her. I mean, anybody who cares and loves any girl will be afraid of proposing. My confidence was boosted by my friends Sameer and Siddharth. They made me comfortable and told me that if she likes you, then it's amazing, but if she doesn't, then its good. At least you would know her real feelings.

Apart of this entire storm in my heart to tell her about my feelings, we continued our private meetings. She was aware that I was developing some feelings for her.

Although we were good friends, but despite knowing that she was into me, it was difficult to propose to her. You know how vulnerable we are at that age.

She didn't come to school for the next three days in a row. First day I missed her a lot because I wanted to talk to her. It didn't happen. The same night, I became anxious. All kind of thoughts were moving in my mind and I was not able to sleep.

The next morning, I woke up with little sleep. I wanted to go to school as soon as possible so that I could meet her. Again, she was absent. I was so anxious that I went out of the class and never returned to class the entire day and wandered around the campus. A lot of things started to revolve in my mind, and believe me, all those feelings were not good. I thought I would never meet her again. I told myself that if she came the next day, I was going to propose to her and tell her what I feel about her – how much she means to me and how much I had missed her.

I was determined to tell her about my feelings, but the next day, she was absent again. I told myself not to worry as she would definitely come the next day.

She did come to school the next day and we chatted alone, but I was unable to tell her about my feelings. So I made my mind to wait until the right moment. Meanwhile, I was enjoying our friendship.

Four months later

I WAS STILL SEARCHING FOR A PERFECT TIME AND place where I could propose to her and tell her that she was the most beautiful girl I had met and that I loved her. That she was the reason why I came to school early and my entire changed attitude. That she was the girl who came in my dreams.

On 3ʳᵈ December 2006, I felt the day had come. It was the computer practical class which used to be a two-period class and took place in a big hall. So I had plenty of time and a perfect corner in the class to propose to her.

You know there is a movie dialogue:

"If you want something whole-heartedly, then all the elements in the universe will help you to get it." The same happened, our computer teacher told me to sit beside her; I was flying high.

I went to sit beside her and was very nervous. I wanted to talk, but I was not able to find the right words. The time was ticking and ten minutes passed. All the confidence, all the machismo was gone. I know we were good friends, but that moment I was like a baby who wanted to speak, but was not able to. I don't know why this happened and I still don't.

Anyhow, around twenty minutes later I spoke, "I want to say something."

She turned to me, blinked her eyes twice and said, "I don't want to talk to you." She turned away.

I was shocked. This was a completely different attitude. She never spoke to me like that and I was looking at her while she was facing the other side.

Once I got my senses back, I asked, "But why?"

She immediately responded, "I don't know and I don't want to talk to you, ever." She then asked her friend to exchange her seat.

I was stunned and remained seated at the same place for the entire class. A lot of thoughts flooded my mind. Why was she angry? Why didn't she want to talk to me? I mean I was just starting a conversation and she responded rudely. And she would not talk with me ever? Why was this happening?

The bell rang to end the computer class and Sameer and Siddharth came to me and asked what happened? Why she had changed her seat?

I narrated the whole event to them. The rest of the day passed by in a blur.

I used to come to school on my bicycle and Sameer would ride pillion. Siddharth was a very sensitive guy. Since I was sad, he wanted to come with us.

We started our journey from school to home walking. I wanted to sit at a quiet place and just relax. So we stopped at our usual samosa shop at Shankar Chowk.

I was quietly seated as Siddharth spoke, "Did you tell her that you love her?"

"No," I said staring at the mild sun.

"Then why did she change her seat?" Siddharth asked.

"I don't know," I said angrily.

Siddharth didn't say anything. Sameer came back with samosas from the counter. He saw me and Siddharth sitting quietly.

"I think you should also stop talking to her. Don't go first and make her feel victorious. She soon will realize what she is missing. Let her come to you," Sameer said in just one breath.

I looked at him and the way it was said. I just said, "Okay."

So I made up my mind not to talk until she approached first. I took this decision at that moment in haste.

The next day, I went to school early as usual and entered the class. She looked at me once and turned her face to the other side. I was not used to this. She used to respond to me with a smile, showing the two perfect dimples on both her cheeks.

Showing her an expressionless face, I went to put my bag on my bench which was just beside the girl's row. I immediately went out of the class to the playing ground where prayers used to take place. I remained there until other students came for the prayer.

Now this routine followed for two weeks. I was getting frustrated. I wanted to talk, but my ego was not letting me do so.

I was known in school as an intelligent student, a sportsman, and a singer. I used to sing during school functions and C.C.A., which was a four period class on Saturday after lunch where students could take part in extracurricular activities.

Since there was no communication between us, I wanted her to know what I meant to say in that computer class. I decided to sing to convey the feelings.

I sang almost all the sad songs I could. I knew somehow through my songs she would get her sense back and would try to talk with me. Over a period of a few days, I must have sang at least fifteen songs. Other students started calling me the king of sadness.

The songs I picked used to have a deep meaning as all sad songs of Bollywood do. Every other student along with some teachers always used to ask me whether I was well or not. The only person whom I wanted to feel those songs was not responding. It was hurting me more than anything.

With each passing day, I was becoming more frustrated, irritated and angry. I had reached nowhere with her or my studies. After forty-five days, my eighth board exam was supposed to happen.

On the eve of 14th January, I was playing cricket. Cricket was the only thing that helped me forget everything. But on that particular evening, I was not focused on my game. Everywhere I looked, her face used to appear in front of me. So I decided on the cricket field that the next day would be the day which would decide the fate of my love.

15th January 2007

MY PLAN WAS TO GO TO SCHOOL EARLY AND WAIT for her to come. When she would arrive, I would take her to a corner and would make her understand my love for her. Everything was going according to plan, as when she entered, only a few students had arrived.

As usual, she glanced at me with a straight face and turned to the other side. This was her daily ritual, so it didn't break my confidence.

I saw her gradually going to her seat and putting her bag down. I moved towards her. She was busy in taking out her notebooks.

I reached her and spoke loudly: "I want to say something."

She looked at me, moved her eyes off me and said, "I don't want to listen."

"But why?"

She looked straight into my eyes. I can't tell you how satisfying that look was. I mean, the continuous ignorance of someone whom you love is painful, and when you get the attention back, you come to existence.

I saw her two big and beautiful eyes getting wet and red. She stood up, held my hand and took me to the corner of the classroom.

"Whatever you wanted to say, you should have told directly to me. Why did you tell Akansha? She will tell everybody about this and I don't want people to say bad things about me. And I certainly don't want my family to know about these things."

When I heard her, I was like, why man? Why didn't you try to talk with her in these forty-five days. I mean, she was upset with me due to this simple reason, and not because of all the other things I was thinking. I felt like killing Sameer and Siddharth because they had suggested I stop talking with her for some time.

"Sorry, but you were not listening to me and Akansha came to me and asked me what happened in the computer class. I was not thinking straight at that time, so I panicked and told her everything I wanted to say to you; so that she could tell you and you'd listen to me again," I said.

"But she is the kind of person who will pass on anything she hears," she said.

"Yes, but you were not listening to me," I said.

By this time, other students had started to flow in the class and it was getting uncomfortable for us. They all were noticing us as they were seeing both of us together after more than a month.

"Let's continue during lunch," she said.

"As you wish."

I was very happy because we had finally talked. I waited desperately for lunch time.

As soon as the bell rang for the fourth period, the period just before lunch, my anxiety started rising. I wanted this period to be over as soon as possible.

The social science teacher started to write the answers of all the questions in the book chapter-wise as our board exams were only one month away. It took exactly thirty-five minutes for him to write all the answers of the same chapter.

I was happy that he was done, but he started to write needless questions which he made up himself from the chapter which had no relation with the board exam.

It was irritating and I was wondering what the fuck was wrong with this guy today.

Finally, after using five minutes of the lunch break, he left the classroom.

I rushed to her bench and the first thing she told me, "What was wrong with sir today?"

"Everything," I said.

We went to the corner of the last bench. Every other student was looking at us like they had never seen us before.

"I want to say something to you," I said.

"I am listening," she said.

I looked right into her eyes and held her hand.

"I love you," I said.

I think I will never be able to describe how numb I felt the moment I proposed to her. It was like everything had come to halt and there were only two people left on the entire planet.

"Listen, you don't know anything about my family. There are so many problems we are facing right now," she said.

She told me about the family fall-out between her father, uncles and her grandfather. She told me about her grandmother being the only family member standing by her father.

"In the midst of all that, if my father hears about this, he will get really mad," she continued.

"You don't worry. I'll help you handle all these problems," I said.

"You know, it's easy to say, but not so easy to do."

Then she narrated a brief story. She told me that a boy from her colony had thrown a love letter in her compound in the evening. Her father was walking and saw the letter thrown in the garden. He picked the letter, read it in front of her, her mother and her brother and directly went to the guy's house. He gave the letter to his father and told the guy, "If I see you doing this again, I will kill you in front of your family."

I listened to her carefully and was stupefied. It was like going through a dark space and seeing your own future.

"You don't worry about it. I am not going to do these stupid things. I love you," I said.

Then she started talking about her family problems again. I do understand that she was troubled, but man, I had just proposed to her and was dying to hear her answer.

"Listen, I still don't have your answer to my proposal," I said.

"I will tell you later, not now," she said and blinked her eyes.

"Take as much time you need," I said.

Suddenly, the bell rang. We entered the classroom and moved to our respective benches. I seriously didn't know which teacher came and went out of the class. I was super blank and was not able to focus on anything.

The only thing which was revolving in my head was her voice and the stories she had told me about her family, but in a good way. Now it was a waiting game for me as she wanted some time to think about it. She must have made up her mind, but you know how Indian girls are; there has to be some drama for every little thing.

17*th* January 2007

I was happy as I had confessed my love to her and now I was waiting for her reply. Although I asked about her decision on the 16th as well, she replied that 'she still had not decided'.

I knew that she was checking my patience.

Finally the day arrived. On the 17th, during lunch I asked her about her decision again.

"So, you must have decided by now?" I said.

"I love you," she said simply.

That was it. That was a moment of joy, a moment of happiness, a moment of relief. I felt like I had achieved something.

"I love you, but I love my family also," she continued.

"I understand," I said.

We both looked into each other's eyes and I could feel the love in her eyes.

"You know, I liked all the songs you sang for me," she said.

"Thank you. But you don't know how difficult that time was for me."

"Yeah I know. It was the same for me too," she said.

All my hard work was bearing fruit and now it was the time for us to enjoy and rejoice all the upcoming moments together.

More importantly, it changed me as a guy, because suddenly, I had become a more responsible one.

23rd January 2007

IT WAS A BEAUTIFUL SUNNY DAY IN SITAMARHI, which is a rarity in winter. All the students who were participating in the republic day function were on the playground.

Shikha and some other girls were also participating. So how in the universe I was supposed to be in class? Although I didn't like to participate in the parade, just to be around her and to get the chance to be alone with her, I also put my name in the probable list of the participants for the parade.

Since our sports teacher was absent on that day, it gave our group the opportunity to play cricket. Shikha and the other girls from our class were sitting across the boundary and were watching us play.

This was not the first time I was playing in front of her. I had played numerous times before and had also won. But this time, it was different; this time I was representing her in front of her friends. I could read her eyes that she wanted me to play well and win.

I was the captain of one team and Sameer was the captain of the other. We played a ten over match. I won the toss and elected to bat first. As usual, I went to open along with Aman.

Aman was short, had blonde hair and was listed in the black list of the school along with me. The black list in our school included the names of those students who were notorious.

I took the strike. Sameer was bowling the first over. I saw her looking at me. I knew if I got out, she would feel embarrassed, and if I hit the first ball for a boundary, Sameer would be under pressure.

Sameer delivered the first ball of the match. I came two steps out of the crease and lofted the ball over. It dropped just beside Shikha and her friends for a six. Her friends stood up in excitement and started jumping and clapping.

She remained seated, slowly clapping and showing off to her friends. It was quite a feminine way of doing it. It was so cute.

We scored 133 runs in ten overs for zero wickets. I scored 62 runs, Aman scored 56 runs and rest was from the extras. Sameer's team scored 116 runs in their attempt.

After winning the match, I went up to where Shikha and her friends were sitting. As a champion, I took her hand, separated her from the herd and went to a quiet place where we could talk uninterrupted.

She had asked me for my childhood photos. So I got some of them from my family album, put them in an album and brought it with me on that day.

"Well played," she said.

"Thank you."

"Well, I brought something for you," I continued

I handed her the album. She smiled with excitement and we settled on the ground.

"Oh wow," she said.

The first photo in the album was that of when I was only one month old in the lap of my grandmother.

"You are naked in it." She pointed out.

"I was just one month old. What do you expect?" I said to justify myself.

"No, I mean you look cute."

"I hope I could get to see some cute photos of you as well," I said looking at her.

First she didn't get it, but when she did, she slapped me on my cheek softly in a girlish manner.

"Why photos?" she said.

I looked at her with excitement as her statement immediately increased the level of testosterone in my body to its maximum point.

"When?" I asked.

"You have to wait for some time for that," she said to douse the fire.

She went through the other photos. There was one photo where my right leg was bandaged and I was lying in the hospital.

"What's up with your leg?" she asked with clear sign of concern on her face.

"Oh that! I had broken my leg on that day," I said.

"What?"

"Yeah, actually I was stuck on the roof of the building in Asansol where one my uncles used to live. I was a great fan of Shaktimaan serial in those days. Since there was no help coming, I jumped off the roof and broke my leg."

"One second, what?" she said with disbelief in her eyes.

"I told you I was fan of Shaktimaan and I was a very naughty child," I said.

"How naughty?"

"Oh my god, you really want to know?" I said

"Yes please," she said.

"Well, when I was four years old, we used to live in Bhagalpur. We used to go to our village for the Chhath festival. I used to give all the prasad to the calves of the cows there."

"And?" she said with excitement.

"Alright, you see these stitches on my nose, beside my nose, and on my head. These all are the small examples," I said.

"So you have broken your head, a leg, and your nose. Anything else?"

"Yes, do you see my right hand?" I said.

"Oh my god, what happened?" she said in shock.

"It's a very interesting story. I was playing cricket in the bedroom. I hit the ball and it went under the bed. I was looking for the ball with the support of my hand. Suddenly someone dropped down on me. It was my brother who was playing *aankh micholi.* I only heard one sound before passing out, and that was the sound of my bone breaking," I said.

I was looking at her. It seemed like she was in my place and was experiencing every moment of the incident.

"Then, why didn't you go to the hospital?" she asked.

"We went to the hospital twice but it never got straight again," I said.

"Didn't you have any problem after that?" she asked.

"No, never. I mean, you saw me playing just now. Did you feel I was in pain?" I asked.

"No," she said, "I love you."

I looked at her; I could see her eyes getting wet.

"Arrey baba, it's alright now," I said and took her hand in mine.

She tapped my leg and then put her arms around me to show her affection.

This was the first time I saw her in tears. You never know how the girl will react to a particular situation and it was her first one in front of me. Before this, I had considered her to be a very strong one, but this incident changed my perception of her. It's always great to have a girl in your life who cares for you.

"Alright, I have some news for you," I said to change her mood.

She looked at me questioningly.

"I love you," I said.

"I know that," she said.

"Good, actually I am going to bring a camera on Republic Day and take some photos together," I said.

"No, you are not," she said.

"I am not asking you; my sister is also performing with her friends," I said.

"But where will we take photos? Everyone will be on the ground along with the principal."

"That you leave up to me," I said.

My sister was also on the ground with her dancing group. Shikha and my sister used to come by the same bus, so they knew each other. My sister saw us together so she came to us and stared at me.

"Meet my friend," I said.

"I know her and I know about you both," she said.

"Good, so you both talk; I am going there," I said and gestured towards my friends.

I left while my sister and Shikha continued their girlish chatting.

As per the plan, I brought the camera on the day of the Republic Day function. The function started with flag hoisting and then the parade.

I felt awkward during the parade but love makes you do certain things which you never expect from yourself.

Then it was time for the main function, which included dancing, singing and other cultural programmes.

Parents were supposed to sit on the chairs arranged behind us. We were supposed to sit in front of the stage on the ground on the mats.

So the first thing I did was to sit beside her. I got that opportunity and we settled beside each other.

"After the function, we'll get some time. It will take twenty minutes for the guests to go, and in between, we can take photos," I said.

"Alright," she said. "Can I ask you something?"

"No, you can't," I said with a smile.

"I remembered, once you said in the class that you want to be a singer. Are you serious about that?" she asked.

"I am serious about that, but I don't think my family is," I said.

"What do you mean?"

"My family is one of a kind. This is not the first thing I want to be," I said.

"Means, they do not support you?" she asked.

"No, I didn't mean that. My family is over protective. They want me to get a job and live a simple and regular life," I continued.

"So what is the first thing you wanted to be?" she asked.

"Alright, when I was seven, I wanted to be an Army officer. I told my parents about this."

"Then?"

"To become an Army officer, I had to join the Army School and my mother didn't want me to go to any other place at that young age," I said. "And you are not supposed to take that decision on your own when you are that young," I continued.

"Oh, I think she did the right thing," she said.

"Do you think so?"

"Otherwise we would not have met," she said with a smile.

"Yeah, but I was very serious about being an Army officer at that time. They used to fascinate me. You know, I got the chance to meet one and I was so happy; for months I used to talk about him," I said.

"Alright, any other dreams of yours?" she asked.

"Oh yes, I wanted to be a cricketer when I was… I think throughout my life. I used to play cricket the whole day in the sun, when most of the kids my age must have been busy playing video games."

"Why didn't you pursue a career in it?" she asked.

"Like I said, my parents want me to get a job. Well, my grandfather was poor. They used to live in the village and had to study in the government school. There was even lack of food in his young days. So whatever he is now is due to his job and he is a very simple man with a simple ideology, and my mother thinks similarly," I said.

"Don't you have any regrets?" she asked.

"Right now, I don't have any regrets. I think if you are talented, you will get to the place you deserve," I said.

My sis and her friends were on the stage for their performance. So I went in front and took photos. I returned to my seat.

"So you know about my dreams, now tell me about yours," I said.

"I don't have big dreams, but I want to be an interior designer," he said.

"Excellent, then you can keep our house well designed," I said.

"Yes, of course."

"We are also here," Keshu said with a laugh and gestured towards other students of our class.

"Hmm!" I said.

We all burst into a laugh and started to talk with each other till the function ended. I saw guests and parents moving towards the parking area to leave. All the other students were standing in the field and took photos.

"Let's go," I said holding her hand.

She hesitated for a moment and then took off with me. We went to the back of the ground and took photos together. We clicked photos with her friends as well. Taking photos in school seemed to be a great deal at that time and we were happy that we did it.

I still have those photos with me, safely kept in the same album which I had showed her. Whenever I see them, they take me back to that moment.

Sports Day

AS OUR BOARD EXAMS NEARED, THE SCHOOL management started extra classes for eighth class students. Students with doubts could clarify them with their respective teachers.

All other classes were off; so it was only eighth class students who were coming to school and due to this reason combined classes were going on. We were getting enough time to cement our relationship. The first sports day was supposed to be held in a few days in our school. All the other schools along with ours were participating.

We were not allowed to participate as our classes were going to continue on the sports day also.

One day, we were allowed to go to the field and watch the matches going on and also to support our school.

The seating arrangement for all the girls was at one end and for boys at a different place. Although it wasn't too far away, I didn't understand the logic behind such a stupid thing.

When we were in the class, we could talk. Now we were sitting apart.

Suddenly it hit me that the whole school was present in the ground; nobody was in the classes. If I managed to take her to the class alone, then we could have some quality time.

There were two problems, first was how to communicate with her and the other was how to take her to the class without anyone seeing us.

To reach our class safely, we had to walk a hundred metres, pass one gate and two guards who were sitting there and were more alert due to the event.

So to solve the first problem, I used gestures.

"Come with me," I gestured.

"What?" she signalled.

"Come with me," I gestured again.

"I can't understand," she gestured shaking her head.

I tried again, but she did not understand.

I gestured to Keshu to come to the water pump, so that I could tell her to send Shikha to our class.

"What happened?" Keshu asked.

"Tell her that I am going to our class and send her there alone," I said.

"Okay," she said with a big smile on her face.

She went to her and whispered in her ear. She smiled and looked at Keshu and then at me.

"No," She shook her head.

"Come," I gestured.

"No," she shook her head again.

I stood up and went towards the main building to our class. I glanced at her to come with my eyes.

Firstly she hesitated, but when she saw me crossing the gate of the ground, she stood up.

I saw her getting up, so I directly went to our class which was in the corner of the second floor and waited for her.

I was watching the guard continuously. I saw her coming to the stairs, but she was with Keshu, not alone. She came into the class with her.

"Keshu, you wait outside the classroom," I said with irritation.

"No Keshu, please don't leave," Shikha said and held her hand.

"I will be waiting outside," Keshu said.

"If you see someone coming up, do inform us," I said.

"Okay," she said and went out.

Only two of us were in that class now. I mean just tell me, how many other couples could have moment like this in their school.

I closed the door partially. I went towards her, took her hand in mine and kissed it. She stood still like a statue.

I moved my left hand in her hair and held her head from the back. As I moved towards her, I could feel her breathing heavily. I kissed her on her forehead first. Then I tilted her head and kissed her on her right cheek in between the dimple.

Then I kissed her on her lips. I could feel her soft lips in between my lips. I was holding her back from my right hand and I could feel her trembling in my arms.

After the kiss, we stood holding hands.

"I want to tell you something," I said.

"I have aids," I said with a serious face. She laughed at first, but when she saw my face, I could see the expression on her face changing to serious. It was so funny and cute to look at her face at that time.

"I am just kidding," I said and burst into laughter.

"Shut up!" she said.

"I have something to tell you," I said.

"What?"

"I might be leaving the school after our board exams," I said.

There was silence and I could see a question mark on her face.

"I was planning to go to Ranchi since last year to complete my studies there. All the arrangements have been made. The reason I am telling you this is because right now, I don't know what to do. I don't want to leave you here alone," I continued.

"Listen, I don't want you to go, but if all the arrangements are made, then you should go. It's completely up to you," she said with a heavy voice.

"I know, but our relationship has just started and I will not be able to talk to you, hear you…," I said.

"Don't worry, we will call each other."

"I will not be able to see you," I said.

"I know. Then don't go. Stay here. You can study here also," she said.

"I can try that," I said.

There was silence again. We were looking into each other's eyes. I took her in my arms, held her tight and leaned to kiss her again.

"I want to tell you something," she said.

"Yeah, tell me," I said.

"I have aids," she said with a serious face.

"Yeah right!" I said with a laugh.

"This is my first kiss," she said.

"Hmm… but you kissed alright," I said.

"How do you know I kissed alright?" she asked.

"Well, I have kissed other girls before," I said.

"Really? How many?" she asked.

"That's not important. The important thing is, this was the best among them," I said.

We stayed holding each other tightly for some more time. Then we got out of the class; she went off with Keshu and I went alone to the playground.

Valentine's Day Celebrations

THIS WAS OUR FIRST VALENTINE'S DAY AS A COUPLE and I really wanted to make it the most special day of her life. So I had a plan and I asked her to cooperate with me. She agreed.

We all know how special Valentine's Day is for lovers, and not just the day, but the whole week.

We made a plan to celebrate it on 13ᵗʰ February as she told me that it would be difficult for her to get out of her house on Valentine's Day for such long duration of time. The police were also alert these days to protect love birds from activists against Valentine's Day. These activists, I believe, are those numbskulls who had zero probability of getting girls so they tried to disturb the love birds and took out their frustration on them.

We planned that she would reach Mehsaul Chowk with Keshu at two in the afternoon in her car. I would be waiting for her and then we would go on my bike. She had told her parents that she would be at Keshu's home, studying for the board exams.

Everything went according to plan as I remained in constant touch with Keshu on the mobile phone. Keshu and Shikha got out of her house and arrived at Mehsaul chowk. Shikha got out of the car and Keshu went back to her house.

The plan was to tell her parents that she was going to Keshu's house and to the driver that she was only coming with us to go to the market.

I was waiting for her at the corner of the chowk standing beside my bike at Mehsaul chowk, one of the busiest chowks of Sitamarhi. I saw her coming out of the silver Santro Xing. She was wearing a light grey suit. Her lean and relatively tall figure looked perfect. She suddenly appeared more mature than me with the same innocence in her body language. I ran to her and gave her the red rose I had brought for her. She also gave me the red rose which she had brought from her garden. I kissed her on her cheek; she hesitated as there were hundreds of people but I didn't care and did the same with the other cheek.

"What are you doing?" she said annoyed.

"What? I am kissing my beautiful girlfriend. I don't care about all of them," I said and gestured towards the crowd.

She shook her head and gestured to go.

We sat on my bike and I took her deep into the city to the places where no one knew us.

"Where are we going?" she asked and put her arms around my stomach and crossed both her hands.

"It's a surprise," I said and smiled.

"But now you can tell me na," she said.

"No."

"Listen, I have told my parents that I will be home by five. Keep that in mind," she said.

"Don't worry about it. You just sit and enjoy," I said.

I drove to the famous pastry shop of Sitamarhi town. They were celebrating Valentine's Day and had made studios of five by five feet area in their shop for couples. I had booked one of the studios. We went inside the hall of the pastry shop. They were still decorating it.

I asked the receptionist to open the studio I had booked for her and to be ready with all the arrangements. We went to the first floor and stopped at one where they had written 'Sudhanshu and Shikha' with white on a red heart shaped balloon which was stickered to the door.

She saw the balloon and looked at me with her eyes wide open; she clapped and jumped in excitement. I knew right away that she had liked the first surprise.

She opened the door and the moment she entered the studio, a shower of red roses welcomed her. She looked at me with a huge smile on her face. I was smiling and was satisfied to see her happy. She spread out both her arms and caught a rose in each.

There was one small table in the room with two bean bags. We sat next to each other and I saw her putting a rose inside her bag. She looked at me.

"This one is for memory," she said smiling.

I blinked my eyes and nodded.

"This was the surprise you were talking about?" she asked.

"Yeah, how is it?" I asked as I wanted to know what she felt about it.

"Amazing, this is the most beautiful surprise I have ever had in my life," she said.

"Well, it's not over yet," I said.

"What?" she said with excitement.

I pressed one of the switches of the switch board and few minutes later a young girl in her twenties came in with the vanilla and chocolate cake. On it was written 'Happy Valentine's Day, my love'. She loved both vanilla and chocolate, so I had told them to make the cake with only these two ingredients. They had completely nailed it.

She saw the cake and got excited like a five-year-old child and hugged me.

We cut the cake and ate it. The waitress was still there, so we invited her to join us and eat the cake with us. Firstly she refused, but when Shikha insisted, she also dug into a slice.

She left with the remaining cake and another came with the smoothies. We took sips of the smoothie and chatted for a while.

They played the song *'Zara si dil mein de jagah tu'* in the background. I held her and we both got up to dance to the song. It was our favourite song.

I could see her eyes getting wet. A drop of tear fell on her cheek and went down passing right between her dimples.

I saw her tears, wiped her face with my hand and kissed her on her cheek.

"Why are you crying? This was supposed to make you happy," I said to change her mood.

"It's just too much to take. I love you." She hugged me very tightly.

"It's okay."

We again sat on our bean bags. But after a few seconds she got up and sat on my lap.

"Thank you," she said.

"No need to thank me. You deserve it, my lady," I said and smiled.

She blinked her eyes and we kissed.

I had booked the place for an hour, so we left soon after. We went outside to tour the city on the bike. At five, I dropped her at the main gate of her colony.

"Will you be coming to school to play Holi?" I asked.

"We will talk about this later," she said before leaving.

I stayed there until she entered her house. I was able to execute the plan successfully so it was a satisfying day for me.

This was our first Holi as a couple. So we had planned to play it together. Our school was closed on that day so we hoped to play Holi on the last day of our extra classes.

We, along with our friends, had planned the last day. I had bought the colors to play with her and our friends.

As soon as we reached school, we were told in the first period that school was over for the day. We were not given the reason for this. So I was very upset with the management.

I had to find a solution for this problem and I did that. I told Sameer to take my bicycle and go. I would be going with Shikha in her bus.

We went to the second last seat of the bus. There were a few students in the bus, so it felt comfortable and private.

There was a twenty-five-minute window for us before my stop. I took some red colour and rubbed it on her cheeks and on both the dimples; she did the same.

"I am going to miss you," she said.

"Same here, but don't worry, we will be calling each other," I said.

"Yes, but there is only one mobile in my house and it's my dad's," she said.

"When your dad comes home after work?" I asked.

"I will call you when he is home. You can't call. I don't want him to know about us," she said.

"Don't worry, I will tell my sis to call you and hand over the phone to me," I said.

"Okay, but take care whenever you call," she said.

"Alright, I will. I can come towards your house," I suggested.

"No, you will not. My father will know about us then," she said.

"Everybody there knows my father. If anybody sees you, we can get into trouble," she continued.

"Okay, as you wish," I said.

Notebook Chat with Shikha (01.05.07)

'My Bhabhi wants to talk to you,' I wrote.

'I can't call you,' Shikha wrote.

'Why?'

'Bas aise he.'

'Kya bas aise he. Explain.'

'I had told you earlier that we will not talk over the phone. I don't like it'.

'How is your dad? Is he alright?'

'Why?'

'*Aise hi, I wanted to meet him*'.

'*Forget it, if you want to see me alive*'.

'*You know yesterday I got fully wet in the rain. My mummy started to tease me with you and my papa was sitting there. She was saying to Johnny (my pet dog) your Bhabhi got drenched.*'

'*Your father didn't say anything?*'

'*Actually he was lying on the bed. He knows that you are my friend. Another day he asked me to call my bahu home so that you could make him tea.*'

'*Tell him to wait for some years.*'

'*Leave him. I am waiting for you to come. You know I have my dinner at 10 p.m. and then I read a book. From 11:30 to 1 a.m., only thing which revolves in my mind is you. Sometimes I get irritated with the thought and end up disturbing Johnny.*'

'*You know you are mad! You don't have breakfast, sleep at 1 in the night, and then you are out of home till late at night if you have fight with your family. From tomorrow, you will have breakfast, will sleep before 12 and will not leave your home after nine in the night. Otherwise don't chat with me.*'

'*Abhi se itna khyal rakhti ho. What will you do later?*'

'*Baad ka baad mein dekha jaega. Now you have to follow these things.*'

'*Okay, but I can't sleep without thinking about you.*'

'*Just imagine that I am near you.*'

'*How?*'

'*In your brain.*'

05.05.07

'*What happened? Explain,*' I wrote.

'*Listen. Tell that ass to stay away from me,*' Shikha wrote.

'*I talked to him. You just don't look at him.*'

Sameer was making funny faces at her and she was annoyed with him. I didn't know what had happened because I had gone out of the class to drink water.

'*I have no interest in that ass. He wants to have a fight with me. If I get angry, then nobody can save him.*'

'*He doesn't want to fight. You just don't get involved in his matter. He is still immature.*'

'*I don't want to get involved, but there is a limit to everything.*'

'*What has he told you?*'

'*I was talking to Shlok at the gate. Avantika ma'am came and told us to go inside. He came and started to speak rubbish. I won't tolerate it*'.

'*You know I love you both. I don't know what to do.*'

'*Listen I am not telling you to choose between me and him. Just keep him away from me.*'

'*I will tell him to stay away from you. Please change the topic.*'

'*On which topic will you give a speech?*'

It was Saturday and C.C.A. was going on in our classroom. We were asked to choose one topic by the teacher and prepare a speech on that topic instantly.

'*On "Young Generation".*'

'*Are you preparing for it?*'

'*Do you think I'll prepare?*'

'*No.*'

'*Hmm… you will speak on which topic?*'

'*I will not speak.*'

'*Why?*'

'*I am not in the mood.*'

'*I will sing a song for you. You choose which song: sing from; a). Tum dil ki, b). Aise na dekho mujhe.*'

'*You sing whichever one you like. Tum jo gaoge achha gaoge.*'

'*You know my sis told my mom that your face looks like Preity Zinta's. So whenever she comes on television, my mom says, 'See it's my bahu'.*'

'*Tell mom that her bahu is not that pretty.*'

'*You know you are more beautiful than her because you are the most beautiful girl I have met in my entire life.*'

'*It's nothing like that.*'

'*You can ask Keshu.*'

'*Jiju, she is one in a billion, isn't she? But I don't understand why she doesn't agree with it?*' Keshu wrote.

'*Not in a billion, but a zillion,*' I wrote.

'*By the way, meri aur apki opinion kafi milti hai; after your marriage with Shikhu, I think we as a pair will blossom. Someone should be on the side of my jiju. Right jiju!*'

I went to give the speech and sang the song '*Aise na dekho mujhe*' on the demand of the students of our class.

'*Nicely sang,*' Shikha wrote.

'*Hmm… you were in front of me, that's why.*'

'*Imagine if I will not be in front of you tomorrow.*'

'*Don't say that. You are mine, you will be with me forever.*'

'*But I will not remain in front of you always.*'

'Why?'

'*Because, summer vacations are coming soon.*'

'*It doesn't matter. I will come to your colony to see you.*'

'*You will not do such a thing. If my mom gets to know about you, then problem ho jaega. Despite the distance, we will remain close by our hearts.*'

Sameer took the copy from me.

'*Sorry, very very sorry,*' Sameer wrote.

Shikha ignored it and didn't write anything back.

'*If he is saying sorry, then what's your problem. He is my friend, just forgive him once,*' I wrote.

'*I know it's my fault. I know I shouldn't have said such things in front of ma'am,*' Sameer wrote.

'*I don't have any intention to fight with you. You come to me to fight and give the pen to Sudhanshu.*'

'*You should forgive him,*' I wrote.

'*It's my decision.*'

'*I am requesting you.*'

09.05.07

'*You know I have bought a ring for you,*' I wrote.

'*I have seen it,*' Shikha wrote.

'*When?*'

'*Kuldeep had shown me a few days ago.*'

'*What? He took it out of my bag?*'

'*Yes.*'

'*I am not gonna leave him now.*'

'*Don't say anything otherwise I will have fight with him and everyone in the class will know about it.*'

'Will you be free on game day?'

'I will not stay alone in the classroom.'

'Then how am I gonna give you the ring.'

'I don't know.'

'Just wait for five minutes so that I can give you the ring.'

'No.'

Why?

'I'm scared.'

'It's ok, now I will give the ring to some other girl.'

'As you wish.'

'Why do you always say no? Once we get married, I will be the boss.'

'Ji nahi! I will be the boss.'

'That depends on me.'

'Why?'

'Because then you will be with me in my arms.'

'Ji nahi! Raaj to mera hi chalega,' she wrote.

'See, I won't be joru ka gulam.'

'I will not let you to be that.'

How?

'Just like that.'

'You love kids?' I asked.

'Yes.'

'How much?'

'As much as you love me.'

'How much do you love me?'

'As much as you love me. More than the freaking world.'

'I wish you could live with me.'

'You had said that sabra ka phal mitha hota hai.'

'Too much sweetness is bad for the health. Till then, it will get rotten'.

'I am what for you. You thought about it?'

'No, I need lot of time?.'

'How much time?'

'Only fifty years.'

'I will not survive for that long.'

'You are gonna live for a thousand years,' she wrote.

'Even an elephant doesn't live that long.'

'You will.'

'On one condition, if you will remain with me for that long,' I wrote.

'Yes I will.'

'Then we will become the oldest living couple of the world.'

'We will become immortal.'

'Hmm… I will come home after recording the songs; you will be waiting for me. I will bring saree for you and then you will wear it and show me'.

'Do you think I will be wearing a saree?'

'Then nighty?'

'Ji nahi, I will wear suit,' she wrote.

'Ok, I will bring suit. Then you will make food for me which we both will eat and after that…'. I wrote.

'I don't know how to cook'.

'I don't know what's up with all the girls. They all say that they don't know cooking. But in my experience, each one of them cooks.'

'It's ok. I will order the food from the restaurant and you will feed me with your hands.'

'That's alright. But who will bring the chocolates?'
'Ok madam! I will open a factory of chocolate for you.'
'Big chocolates!' She wrote.
'Cadbury or Nestle?' I wrote.
'Cadbury.' She wrote.
'Ok, ask Keshu. How she has three eyes,' she wrote. The bell rang and school got over for the day.

11.05.07

'Arrey! This is all Kuldeep and Ankur's doing. They are trying to create problems between us so that we get separated,' I wrote.

'Main bi dekhti hun ki kaun kya kar leta hai. It's not easy to separate us,' Shikha wrote.

Actually Kuldeep and Ankur told her that they have seen me with another girl the previous Sunday near Shankar Chowk. She was looking really upset.

'Then why are you upset. Smile now.'

'I don't want to.'

'You have to because someone lives to see you.'

'Don't be sad, I am happy. As long as you are with me I don't want anything,' she wrote.

'Hmm… problem no: 2. when is Saurabh coming?'

She had told me earlier that Saurabh was the son of her father's friend who liked her and wanted to marry her. And it could be a real deal as they were good family friends.

'Don't know. Bas kuch din mein hi tapkega,' she wrote.

'Lamba hai safar petrol kam hai
Lamba hai Safar petrol kam hai
Shikha ki maa patakha toh

Sudhanshu ka baap bum hai,' I wrote to change her mood.

'Wow, very nice. Wah Wah!'

'Okay be ready for tomorrow. Last time I fulfilled your demand, now it is your turn.'

'I will not sing.'

'I am not asking you to sing. You just be prepared for tomorrow.'

12.05.07

'You know, whenever I get stuck practising any song, I think about you. I start to feel better,' I wrote.

'It's not me, it's you. You are a good person. If you ever feel alone in your life, think about me, and I will be there for you, and one more thing, from tomorrow, have lunch. I shouldn't have to remind you again."

'Okay, when I become hundred and sixty-five kilos, then don't try to run away.'

'I will not run. Tum khate hi kitna hoge.'

'Very less, little more than your brother.'

14.05.07

'Why you are drinking chilled water? You will get sick,' I wrote.

'That's why I am drinking it,' Shikha wrote.

'It will be a problem for your dad.'

'Let it be. Why is it bothering you?'

'He is like my dad. It should bother me.'

'You do your duty and I will do mine.'

'Hmm… what I am for you? You thought?'

'*I told you earlier. It will take thirty years.*'

'*I have also started to watch WWE fights,*' I wrote to make her jealous.

'*You can watch that. Nothing happens just by watching.*'

'*Hmm…. I liked it.*'

'*Continue watching. I like Harry Potter.*'

'*What is so interesting about that chashmish? Real fun is in watching girls fight.*'

'*Don't call him chashmish. He is beautiful, smart, dashing, brave and famous.*'

'*I agree with you, but chashmish must be having difficulties in seeing you properly.*'

'*Ji nahi, Harry Potter is Harry Potter.*'

'*Hmm… Chunky Pandey is Chunky Pandey.*'

15.05.07

'*You don't have your lunch and ask me to eat,*' I wrote as I saw her outside the classroom throughout the lunch period.

'*I always do. Who told you I don't?*'

'*Keshu.*'

'*She lied.*'

'*Hmm… I had to make my lunch today, for your sake.*'

My parents were in Kota with my brother, so I had made my own lunch that morning.

'*Toh kya ho gya. Boys should make their own lunches.*'

'*Yeah right! Today is the 15th. Where is problem no: 2?*'

'*Who knows if he has arrived by now?*'

'*Tell him to meet me first.*'

'*Okay, I will try, but let him come first.*'

'You have to, and one more thing, don't let him get near you.'

'I will talk the whole day with him.'

'That I know; you will not go near him.'

'I will.'

'Hmm… then you must invite me for your wedding.'

'Do you think I will not invite you? I will invite you to the other ceremonies as well,' she wrote.

'Hmm… then listen to this:

Phoolon ka ambar laga denge

Tere ghar bhi bahar la denge

Tum jo na mili hamko

Duniya ko shamashhan bana denge.

Now you understand.'

'Yeah I understand. You have to come with your family now. I will send the invitation card.'

'Don't worry, madam. I will come with my thirteen wives and twenty-six children. Just make good arrangements for us.'

'Yeah, on the terrace.'

'Where will you have the mandap? In the washroom?'

'Tumse matlab?'

'Honeymoon in a garage?'

'Why'll I tell you?'

'Ok, happy married life to you. Ja bewafa ja hame pyaar nhi karna.'

'Bye bye.'

'Achha sila diya tune mere pyaar ka….'

'How many times you are gonna sing this song? Now I am bored.'

'You are bored? There are so many girls in our school who are crazy about this song.'

'*Hmm… leave them. I am bored.*'

'*Anyway, so how's your plan for the future going on with your brother?*'

'*Who told you that he is my brother?*'

'*I just know that he is your brother and my saala.*'

'*He is my first love.*'

'*Listen, if he is your first love then you should marry him.*'

'*As you wish.*'

'*That means you will marry your brother?*'

She scratched out the 'brother' and wrote 'love' in place of my above statement.

'*I didn't say that. He is my hero in reel life and you are my hero in real life. Never compare yourself to him.*'

'*Why will I compare myself with chashmish? He is your first love na?*'

'*He is nothing to me.*'

'*You know nothing means husband sometimes.*'

'*No it doesn't.*'

'*See, while discussing all this rubbish, I forgot to tell you that today is my parent's marriage anniversary.*'

'*Wow, wish them from my side.*'

'*Hmm… Papa was out since the last three days and yesterday he came when I was sleeping and went out before I woke up.*'

'Wish him tonight or you can wish him on the mobile.'

'*Okay, by the way we will marry in winter,*' I wrote.

'*That will be decided by our elders.*'

'*I will force them to have it in winter.*'

'*It solely depends on them.*'

'*I am coming to your house tonight with the baraat.*'

'*Come soon.*'

'Are you sure? You don't know me I will come with no hesitation.'

'Come na, everybody will think a pagal has come from a pagalkhana.'

'Hmm… to take his pagli.'

'I will not be at my home today. I am going out with my family for dinner.'

'Where?'

'I will not tell you.'

'I knew you will never tell me,' I wrote.

'Then why did you ask?'

'Just for formality.'

'I will never tell you anything.'

16.05.07

'Why do you help me? It will make me a more bigda hua bachcha,' I wrote.

'I don't like any complaints in your diary. By the way, why didn't you do your homework first?' Shikha wrote.

'Koi nahi, I will fill your diary with complaints too.'

'First, I will let you fill your diary, only then na.'

'Great! That's my girl. Now I will never do my homework.'

'Then I will hide your diary and you will be beaten by the teachers.'

'Means you will let the teachers beat me?'

'See, I can't beat you. Then I can make sure that you must get beaten by the teachers.'

'You can beat me. I will say nothing because it will never hurt me.'

'My hands are very solid.'

'Alas! The day will come when you will beat me with your soft hands. I will love every second of it,' I wrote.

'Listen, your mom has already given me permission to beat you. That day is not too far when you will get a solid one from me.'

'When you will beat me, it will feel like a two-year-old child is kissing me.'

'Until now, you have not been beaten by me.'

'Believe me, I am waiting.'

'Hmm… wait.'

'The day will come soon.'

'I am also waiting.'

'It will come soon.'

'Ten years later,' she wrote as soon as she understood.

'It means you said yes.'

'No.'

'What do I have to do for your consent.'

'Wait.'

'Till when?'

'I am majboor.'

What majboor?

'Jaan kar anjaan mat bano,' she wrote.

'It's not majboori. It's your stupidity,' I wrote.

'But for me it is.'

'Are you happy about it?'

'What do you think?'

'Means?'

'Whatever you will think will be right?'

'*I think about every prospect. In fact, I have other girls in mind.*'

'*Then what do I care?*'

'*Nothing. then you have to wait.*'

'*You will never do such things.*'

'*You have that much faith in me?*'

'*Yes.*'

'*It means you said yes.*'

'*No.*'

'*By the way, you know yesterday I was watching a fight between Leta and Victoria. Have to say Leta is awesome. My saala watched it or not?*'

'*No, he has now become a nice guy. By the way, the Rock is really handsome.*'

'*He is rubbish.*'

'*Are you jealous of him?*' she wrote.

'*Why do you think I am jealous of him?*'

'*You are jealous.*'

'*Why will I be. When I will show you my body then you will become my fan,*' I wrote.

'*Let's see whose body is better,*' she wrote.

I read it and unbuttoned two buttons of my white school shirt to showed her my body in class while the teacher was writing something on the black board. She became shy and gestured to me to stop.

Uncle's Wedding

THE ONE MONTH LONG SUMMER VACATION WAS over. So we had hardly spent time together. It was not enough for us to just talk on the phone. It was now time for us to take out our frustration.

But, just after the classes started, I had to go to Ranchi to attend my youngest maternal uncle's wedding. I hadn't told her about this before, so I was looking for the right time to tell her about my absence in the coming days.

The wedding was on 26th June and the Matkor ceremony was on 25th June. Our train was on Sunday night. So I decided to talk with her on Saturday 23rd as after lunch we would have ample time together during C.C.A.

"I am going to Ranchi to attend my uncle's wedding," I said.

"When is it?"

"On the 26th," I said.

"July?" she asked.

"No, this month," I said.

"Then, when are you going?"

"We have our train tomorrow," I said.

"And you're telling me now!" she said in anger.

"Hmm… if I would have told you earlier, you would have stopped me from going," I said.

"When will you return?" she asked.

"I don't know yet. We are very close as a family so we may have to stay back a few days."

"But try to come as soon as possible," she said.

"I will try my best, but I might not be able to change their decision," I said.

"I am nobody?" she said rolling her eyes.

"I didn't say that. It's just that you need to be around your family during these times," I said.

"Hmm, by the way, what does your uncle do?"

"He is in a private company working as a utility manager in Ahmadabad," I said.

"Wow, it's a beautiful place," she said.

"You have been there?" I asked.

"No, we actually went to see Somnath Mandir in Verawal. We stayed there one night as our train was the next day. It's a huge temple by the seashore," she said.

"Hmm…" I said.

It's truly a coincidence that I went to college in Gandhinagar and got my first job in Ahmadabad. You never know where these connections are made. But when they happen, they just make you believe in destiny.

"Will you miss me?" she asked.

"No, I will be busy enjoying the wedding," I said.

She looked at me with anger and started to walk away. I held her hand.

"I don't want to miss you; the moment I will start missing you, I will leave everything and come here. I want to make you my strength, not my weakness," I said.

"I know, but I am gonna miss you. We had been apart for a month and now again I will not be able to see you."

"What did I tell you now?" I said.

"Ohkk, enjoy yourself and stay away from other girls," she said coyly.

"I will try my best, madam," I said and smiled.

"Hmm... do you want anything from there?" I added.

"Yes, you," she said.

"That you already have. Anything else?"

"I would like to see the wedding pics," she said.

"Okay, whatever pics I will take with my cell phone, I will show you."

"I am thinking I will also not come to school," she said.

"Why?" I asked.

"You will not be here. So I will get bored," she said.

"No, don't do this. You carry on with your classes. It's important," I said with a smile.

"And on Monday, there will be a surprise for you," I added.

"Really, what kind of surprise?" she said firstly with excitement and then with suspicion.

"Well, it's a surprise, so can't tell you," I said.

"Okay. Don't," she said.

"Well, it's been sometime since our last kiss," I said.

"Well, add more time to that," she said.

"Oh come on, just one for memory," I said.

"No, no, you are not getting any," she said.

"Okay, I will get kisses from girls there," I said with irritation.

"Go ahead, but today you are not getting any," she said with a huge smile on her face.

"It will be raining kisses there," I said.

"Oh, best of luck," she said, still smiling.

I took her in my arms and kissed her on her lips. I didn't care who was watching. After the kiss she looked at me with disbelief on her face.

"There you go!" I said proudly.

She smiled and at the same time felt shy in front of the other students of our section who were looking at us with their eyes wide open in complete shock.

I wrote the letter to Shikha and handed it to Shlok and asked him to give it to her on Monday.

Dear Shikha,

When you will be reading this letter, I will be in Ranchi. I didn't tell you, but god, I have started to miss you already.

Yes, this is the surprise about which I told you earlier. I am not much of an expressive guy, but the thing is, I love you.

I hope it will keep you engaged till I come back. It is very old fashioned to write a letter, but a sweet way to express my feelings for you, I thought.

I am giving this letter to Shlok so he must have given you the letter.

This is the first love letter I am writing for you, so this one is special for me. I have heard from someone that it is better to live in separation for some time because it makes you realize how much you love each other and also to strengthens your bonding. I hope it will work for us.

I want to continue writing, but I will not. Otherwise I will not stop.

Love you!
Sudhanshu

It was around eight in the morning on 27th June. I and my cousin brother were sitting at the bride's house in Tharpakhna in Ranchi. The last few functions were going on in the living room before the bidai.

We were surrounded by the ladies of the bride's house. I was awake since the past thirty-eight hours. There was so much chaos around now and it was irritating me on so many levels.

I asked my brother to give me his phone so that I could talk with Shlok and ask him about her. I dialled his number knowing that he would be getting ready for school.

"Hello?" Shlok's mother said from the other side.

"Hello aunty, this is Anand. Is Shlok there?" I said.

"Yes beta," she said and handed the phone to Shlok.

"Hello," Shlok said.

"Did you give the letter to her?" I asked.

"Yes, I gave it to her yesterday," he said.

"What did she say?" I asked.

"Nothing, she just took the letter," he said.

"Tell her that I had called you and also that I miss her."

"Okay brother, I will."

"Thanks."

Mansi

IT WAS A RAINY SUNDAY.

We were asked by Rishikesh sir to come around nine in the morning for a class of Sanskrit grammar. He was going to teach us 'Shandhi Vichhed' from the Bihar board grammar book of Sanskrit.

Well, Rishikesh sir was the co-owner of our coaching institute and he used to teach Sanskrit. He was a bald, short guy, who used to wear a cap all the time, just to feel confident.

He was a great teacher. He used to teach difficult sections from the Bihar board grammar book to us so that we could easily solve the questions of our C.B.S.E. textbook.

I was sitting in my regular seat which was just beside sir's. I had the view of the outside through the huge netted windows.

I saw a tall girl with long hair coming in the direction of our coaching centre. She was wearing a sky blue coloured top and a denim skirt. I could see her confusion about where to place her foot as there were water puddles everywhere. I wished at the same moment, please god, send this girl to my class.

The office was just beside our class so I got the opportunity to see her closely while she was going towards the office. I could see her relatively small eyes and it looked tempting even in that single glance. It's amazing how some memories get stuck in your mind with impossible details.

She was with a middle-aged man who went directly to the office. So Rishikesh sir also went towards the office which was separated by a bookcase from our classroom. I could easily hear the ongoing discussion between them.

"What subjects do you teach here?" the man asked.

"We teach all the subjects which are being taught in the school," Rishikesh sir said.

"What subject do *you* teach?"

"I teach Sanskrit," sir said. "We have different teachers here for different subjects," he added.

"How many students in one batch?" the man asked.

"Eight to ten students in a batch."

"It must be hard to focus on a single kid if there are many students in a batch?" the man asked the tricky question.

"No, no, it's better for them as it will enhance their competitive nature and they will progress with each other's help."

"See someone gave me a reference of your coaching centre. I will not be here as I live in Patna and I want a place where she can learn freely," the man said.

"Don't worry, we will try to give her as much attention as we can, though it is the student who is responsible for their success," sir said.

"Wait for a minute," sir excused himself.

He came into our room and told us to leave. The girl and the man were still in the office. I wanted to get one more glimpse of her so I waited outside the main gate.

I purposely involved the other students in a discussion so that I didn't look desperate.

The funny thing was that we stood there for around twenty minutes, but still there was no sign of her coming outside.

It was getting late. So at last I left the coaching centre and went with Sameer and Vinay to have a snack. Vinay was the guy from my section, a new friend of mine who had joined our school this year. There was a sweet shop at Shankar Chowk that used to sell *litti* in the morning.

We sat down and asked the waiter to bring three plates of litti with extra *chokha*. The waiter knew us as we were the regulars, so the next moment we had our orders with us.

"Did you see that girl?" Vinay said out of nowhere.

"Which girl?" I said innocently.

"The girl who came to our coaching today."

"Oh yes," I said.

"Yes, the tall one," Sameer said and smiled.

I laughed as Vinay was a short guy and it appeared that he was interested in her. So to remind him that she is taller than him, Sameer had said this.

"So what if I am short? Salman Khan is also a short man," he said in defence as we laughed.

"Jokes apart, she really looked good," Sameer said.

"Hmm…" I said.

"What do you guys think? Will she join our class?" Vinay asked me.

"Arrey, yes man, she will come to our class. Don't worry," I said.

"Thanks man," Vinay said with a smile.

I used to enter the classroom late during coaching classes. On Wednesday in the same week when I reached, Vinay was waiting for me outside the main gate with a huge smile on his face.

"You are alone here. Where are others?" I asked him as we'd all gather near the gate before going into class.

"They have not arrived yet," he said, still smiling.

"What happened? Why are you so happy? I asked.

"She's in our class," he said.

"She, she who?" I asked.

"That girl man."

"Which girl man?" I asked clueless.

"The tall one!"

It was really good news. I became excited and thanked god for sending at least one pretty girl to our class.

"If she is inside, then what are you doing here?" I asked.

"She is alone. So I came outside so that I wouldn't look desperate," he said.

"Really nice thought, brother. And you wonder why you are single," I said.

"If you don't approach her, then how will you woo her?" I added.

"Oh yes, I thought that, but I got nervous and came out of the class," he said.

"Don't worry champ, one day you will," I said and tapped his shoulder.

Soon everyone else arrived. We all went into the class room together. There were thirteen of us studying at that time.

Our seats were fixed. Sameer and I used to sit beside each other; Amrita, Kamini, and Preeti sat in one row starting just beside Sameer's seat perpendicularly and the rest used to sit behind us.

Amrita, Kamini and Preeti were all from our school. Amrita was a tomboy. Kamini and Preeti, on the other hand, were proper Bihari girls who were short and feminine.

Amrita saw the new girl sitting on her seat and got pissed off. She took her bag and kept it on her lap and told her that the seat was hers.

The new girl calmly did what Amrita wanted. She took her bag and sat down just in front of my seat.

Throughout the class, neither did she say anything, nor did anybody try to start any sort of conversation with her.

As soon as class was over, she took her bag and left. I wanted to know where she came from, but she ran like a bullet.

I had a feeling after the way Amrita behaved with her, and that nobody tried to talk with her, and with the determination she left, she would not return for classes.

Vinay was determined to find out where she comes from. He went fter her like another 'short' bullet.

The next day, I came late and class was over. I saw her sitting in the same seat which was in front of mine.

My seat was vacant as nobody took my chair, not because I was the king or something, but because everybody used to feel comfortable in their own chairs.

She followed the same routine as the first day. She remained in her seat, didn't try to talk with others and nobody spoke to her as well. She went out of the coaching again as soon as class was over.

Soon, we were chilling at the parking area.

"Who is she?" I asked Kamini and showed an emotionless face.

"I don't know," she said.

"Why doesn't she talk with you all?" I asked.

"She remains alone and maintains a distance from us."

"Ohk…" I said.

As usual, Sameer, Vinay and I went together to our regular samosa shop at Shankar Chowk.

"You went after her yesterday?" I asked Vinay.

"No," he said.

"Come on, man. I saw you leaving the classroom as soon she left," I said.

"Oh yeah, I thought nobody had noticed me," he said with a smile. "Well, I went to see where she lives. She lives in Sameer's colony at the corner of the road," he added.

"What? She lives in my colony?" Sameer said.

"Yes, the corner house at the start of the street in which you live," he said.

"But I've never seen her there," he said.

"She must be a shy girl who stays indoors," I said.

"But I'd have known her if she is living in my colony."

"It's okay man, now you know. Go find out who she is," I said.

"Please Sameer bro, find out about her," Vinay said.

"Don't worry bro, I will interrogate her tomorrow," I said.

❖

"Excuse me," I said.

She was sitting in front of me and although she heard my voice, she didn't respond.

"Yes, I am talking to you," I said to remove her confusion.

She turned towards me, with a question mark on her face.

"Hi," I said.

"Hi," she said with a question mark still on her face.

"What's your name?" I asked.

"Mansi."

"You are new here?" I asked.

"Yes, my family moved from Patna last month," she said.

"Which school are you from?" I asked.

"R.A.V. school."

"Our school?" I said surprised.

"I don't know your school," she said.

"I mean, we study in R.A.V. and we never saw you there."

"I told you I am new here."

"Oh, I forgot," I said.

"Okay, what's your name?" she asked.

"Sudhanshu. Well, I saw you not talking to anyone so I thought I'd break the ice," I added.

"Oh, thanks."

"You can talk with everyone. We don't bite, and if you have any problem, you can talk to me," I said.

"Okay," she said with a smile.

I wanted to make her comfortable because I could relate to her. My father is a government officer and after every three or six years, we used to get transferred to a new place.

Aakriti and Kurtika

AS I ENTERED THE CLASS THE NEXT DAY, I SAW TWO
new girls sitting with the other girls.

I immediately recognized one of them. She was Aakriti. I
was seeing her after ages. She had been in the same section with
me in the fifth standard when she was in our school. I heard from
some other student that she had failed in the seventh standard
and had left our school.

She was looking better than the last time I saw her. She was
thin and tall and had beautiful long hair. She had big round eyes
which complemented her new look.

The other girl Kurtika was relatively shorter in height than
Aakriti. She was remarkably fair and had blue eyes; she could
pass off as a foreigner.

Rishikesh sir came in and saw the two new girls sitting in
the class.

"What are your names?" he asked to both of them.

"Aakriti"

"Kurtika."

"Today is your first day in the class?"

"Yes sir."

"How did you come to know about our coaching class?" he asked.

This was his favourite question to every new student.

"Mansi told me. She is my sister," Aakriti said.

She was looking at me to get my reaction when she said that she was her sister. I immediately understood that this is the reaction of the action of me approaching Mansi.

After the class was over, Aakriti came to me along with Kurtika. Mansi was standing in the corner and was watching us talk.

"Hi," Aakriti said.

"Hi. How are you?"

"I am good. How are you?"

"I am also good," I said.

"Where you have been?" I asked.

"Oh, after seventh class, I changed my school," she said.

I knew the reason of her leaving the school but just to make her comfortable, I didn't bring it up. "She is your sister?" I said and gestured towards Mansi.

"Yeah, she is my cousin. She told me that a guy named Sudhanshu was asking her questions. So I had the suspicion that it was you," she said smirking.

"Ok, actually I was making her comfortable. She used to sit alone and not talk to anybody, so I decided to break the ice," I said.

"Yeah, she is the quiet one," she said and looked towards her.

"Hmm… Oh my god I can't believe I am talking to you," she said.

"Why?" I asked.

"Arrey, you used to be a notorious guy back then and I used to fear you," she said.

"What fear? I just used to enjoy myself and have fun in the class," I said.

"I still remembered that you was the monitor of the class and used to top the class. At the same time, you used to tease all the girls in our class," she said in shear excitement.

It's always nice to hear about yourself. And I really was happy to hear that I had made an impact on someone's memory.

"Hmmm… you remembered all those things?" I said.

"Yes. I think everyone from our class would be remembering each and every thing about you. You were a character then," she said.

"She is really beautiful," I said and gestured towards Mansi.

"You will never change, will remain the same," she said and shook her head.

"I am just paying a compliment," I said and smiled.

"Hmm, I know you." She looked at me with rolling her eyes.

Kurtika was listening to us. I asked Aakriti about her and she told me that she studied in the same class in the same school with her and she also lived in her colony.

I gestured towards Mansi and asked her to join us.

"You told them about yesterday?" I asked her.

"I wanted to know whether she knows you or not," she said with hesitation.

"It's okay. Since they are here, now you can have fun," I said.

"You are beautiful and I think you will look more beautiful when you interact with other people," I said.

"Thanks. I will make sure that I look more beautiful," she said and rolled her eyes knowing that I was flirting with her.

Notebook Chat with Shikha (18.07.07)

'Ek baat bolein, I am not feeling good since the last two days. I have a feeling that something bad is going to happen,' Shikha wrote.

'What? Congrats,' I wrote.

'I am serious.'

'Nothing will happen to you. Don't worry, I am with you na. Some guy following your bus?'

'No.'

'What's your weight?'

'21125 kilos.'

'Is there a truck in your body?'

'No, an airplane.'

'How many seats in it?'

'Only one,' she wrote.

'What I will do alone in there?'

'It's only for you,' Keshu wrote.

'No, it's only for Harry Potter,' Shikha wrote.

'What will you do with your brother?' I wrote.

'Listen, bhai hoga tumhara, mera toh boyfriend hai.'

'Hmm... boyfriend. I am going on a honeymoon with Katrina.'

'Go stupid, I have the dashing Harry Potter.'
'No one is sexier than Katrina.'
'Hmm… where is she? I can't see her.'
'That's why I ask you to not think about that chashmish. You also need a chashma now.'
'I see much better than you.'
'Then tell me what you see in me?'
'A lean, thin and stupid ass.'
'Gadhe se pyaar kar liya.' I wrote.
'Yes, what can I do! Love is blind.'
'Give your ass a flying kiss.'
'No.'

19.07.07

'You wanted to say something?' I wrote.
'Nothing,' Shikha wrote.
'It's been too long now. Tell me what I am for you?'
'Stupid, idiot, gadhe, bhulakkad, Ranchi returned and Mr Old man.'
'Mrs Idiot, stupid, bhulakkad, gadhe, Ranchi returned and Mrs Old man, bas itna hi sochi?'
'Listen you can't copy me.'
'I just repeated your words.'

07.08.07

'Why is she upset?' I wrote to Keshu.
'Who told you that I am upset, stupid?' Shikha wrote as she took the copy from Keshu.

'I can see it clearly, Mrs Stupid.'

'Hmm… go check your eyes.'

Why didn't you tell me that it was Keshu's birthday last week?'

'I didn't get the time. You should have remembered it since she is your friend as well, bhulakkad.'

'I must have forgotten'.

'Ho he bhulakkad'.

08.08.07

'You also have participated in parade?' I wrote.

'I am going to anchor this time,' Shikha wrote.

'You don't come to me as it disturbs your study. Now it will not be disturbed?

'No'.

'I might not come on 15th August.'

'Why?'

'I will get bored since you will be busy.'

'Okay, don't come,' she wrote.

'Hmm…'

This was the last copy chat between us.

Me and Mansi

MANSI STOOD UP AND TOUCHED THE FEET OF Rishikesh sir and handed a slab of chocolate to him.

"Sir, it's my birthday today," she said.

"God bless you. Happy birthday," he said.

We all started to sing happy birthday loudly and clapped to wish her on this special day.

After the class got over, she went to each student and gave them chocolates. She came to me and handed me a chocolate.

"I don't eat Dairy Milk chocolates," I said.

"Why?" She asked.

"I don't like it," I said.

"Okay, tell me which chocolate you like?" she asked and put the dairy milk in her bag with the rest of the chocolates.

"It's okay, Mansi. Happy birthday!" I said and extended my hand to shake hands with a smile on my face.

"Thank you, but tell me which chocolate you like," she said.

I paused to look at her. She was really earnest.

"5 star," I said.

She stopped distributing chocolates immediately and sped out of the class. I wondered if I had upset her. I should have taken the chocolate and later I could have given it to Vinay. Few minutes later, she returned.

"There you go. Happy!" She said handing me a 5 star while still panting.

"Did you…?" I asked and gestured outside.

"Yeah!" she said.

"Happy birthday!" I said.

I was really touched. This changed my perception towards her and I started to take care of her.

20th August 2007

Mansi now had started to come to me and used to clarify her doubts with me. I was still the smartest one in our class. Amrita had been absent since the last two days. So Mansi started to sit beside me for my supervision.

Mansi was asking me about her doubts from the S. Chand book of Chemistry. Amrita entered the classroom and her eyes met Mansi's. I was also looking at Amrita; I could see her face getting red in anger, and her eyes burning out of jealousy.

She came towards us and stood in front of Mansi.

"Get up!" she bossed over.

Mansi paused for a few seconds in which she looked at me first, then at the notebook and then at Amrita.

"Just a minute," she said and gestured with her finger.

"No, get up right now," Amrita said and took Mansi's bag and put it on the ground, held her hand and started to pull her off that seat.

It all happened very fast and had turned ugly.

"What are you doing?" I held Amrita's hand and tried to make her leave Mansi's.

"This is my seat," she said in a heavy voice as though she'd break down in tears, and let go with a jerk.

"Go sit on that seat," I shouted at Amrita and gestured towards the bench which was at the farthest corner of the class.

She immediately turned in anger, threw her bag on the corner bench and got out of class.

I looked towards Mansi.

"Are you okay?" I asked.

"Yes! You shouldn't have shouted at her," she said politely.

"You saw her behaviour," I said in a reasonably loud voice.

"Now she will never talk to me again," she said.

"She is an idiot," I said and sat.

She also sat down.

"You don't know, it was my fault that I was on her seat," she said.

"What?" I asked in anger.

She looked right into my eyes.

"Nothing," she said.

She remained on the same seat that day, but changed her seat from the next day.

Teacher's Day

AFTER CELEBRATING IN SCHOOL, NOW IT WAS TIME to celebrate teacher's day in our coaching class, although it was not planned earlier.

So after the function in school, Sameer came to me and asked me whether we should celebrate it in the coaching class as well.

"They will not allow us to have any kind of function," I said.

"Why?" he asked.

"You know them man! Both of them are frustrated with us and they will not allow us as they would think that we will do some notorious activity again," I said.

"Nah, Bihar board guys are celebrating today," he said.

"What?" I said in disbelief.

"Yes, they had planned very early and Rajesh sir and Rishikesh sir had given permission to them," he said confidently.

"How in hell did they give them permission, yar? I mean they never give permission to us to do any function," I said in anger.

"Exactly," he said.

"Wait, we are goanna celebrate today in coaching also," I said.

"But, right now, I have no money with me," he said.

"That you leave up to me. I will take care of it," I said.

"Okay," he said.

We planned to reach the coaching classes early so I told Sameer to inform Kamini about it, as she could call the other girls and inform them. I took the responsibility of calling the boys and inform them about our plan.

As planned, I reached early and saw that major parts of the classrooms were already decorated by the students of Bihar Board School. But they had left our classroom undecorated. It was sad and at the same time ridiculous behaviour by them. Gradually, we all accumulated there. We went to Rishikesh sir and Rajesh sir in the office to get permission to celebrate teacher's day. Rajesh sir was the co-owner of the coaching centre along with Rishikesh sir, again a tall, bald man with fair skin.

"Sir, we also want to celebrate teacher's day," I said.

"But why? Bihar board students are celebrating it, you all can join them," Rishikesh sir said.

"No sir, we want to celebrate in R.A.V. style," Amrita said.

"But do you have that much time to plan, prepare and execute it?" Rajesh sir said with concern.

"Sir, you just give us the permission, we will handle the other things," I said.

"Ok, but where will you do it?" Rajesh sir asked.

"We will do it in our class," Kamini said.

"No, don't decorate that classroom; you can do in the last room," Rishikesh sir said.

"But there are benches in that room," Shubham said.

"Yes, there are, but you have to do it in the last room," he said.

"Okay, we will celebrate it in that room," I said.

We gathered in our classroom to plan what preparation would be needed.

I obviously was leading the function. Everyone was welcome to pitch in with suggestions and I was going to take the final decision.

The first hurdle was to clean the room for the party. As we opened the room, we got a clear view of how dirty that room was. There were dead insects, cobwebs and broken benches. The light bulb was missing as well. There was a lot to be taken care of.

It was a set up by Rishikesh sir to get the room cleaned. We were aware of it, but I think the idea and passion of celebrating made us brush it aside.

We divided the team for the cleaning, decoration, and for food. I asked the students to contribute some money as well.

We hadn't told them in advance to bring money. They gave whatever money they had, but it was short by a huge margin. So I told them that I am going home to bring the remaining amount for the expenses.

As I was going towards the parking area to take my bicycle, I was stopped.

"Listen, wait!" Mansi shouted.

I turned and saw her coming towards me in a hurry.

"Bring your sister with you," she said with a smile.

"But how am I going to bring her on this bicycle?" I asked.

"Oh okay, no problem," she said with her head down.

I saw her excitement changing to disappointment. But I had so much on my mind at that time, that I didn't say anything. My home was one kilometre away from the coaching centre; it took me five minutes to get there on the bicycle.

I saw my uncle's bike parked in the garage. My mom told me that he had gone to work with a colleague today.

I took some of the pocket money I had saved and asked my sis if she wanted to come and celebrate with us. She said yes, and it was expected, as she was doing nothing at home.

Back at the coaching, I could see that Sameer and Devesh were already half way through shifting the benches. Devesh was not from our school but was an intelligent student and a very nice friend.

Mansi saw my sis and she almost jumped from her seat and took my sis into her arms and hugged her. I was aware that they liked each other's company, but it was unexpected to see them jumping and shouting like two old cats. Both of them settled beside each other.

As assigned by me, Sameer and Vinay were supposed to buy the snacks. Shubham started to prepare for his anchoring while Devesh, Amrita, and Kamini went to buy the decorative items from the shop just outside the campus. Mansi, Aakriti and Kurtika were supposed to clean the room.

We also decided to have a small function which would include dancing by Amrita, and a song by Preeti and Kamini. Vinay was going to sing a Christmas song.

I went to buy the snacks along with Sameer and Vinay on the bike. The idea was to bring all the necessities soon so that we all can be together most of the time, and could enjoy the moment.

As I went towards the parking area, someone held my hand from behind in the passage. It was Mansi.

"Thank you," she said with a smile.

You know, there was something about that girl, even the way she said 'thank you'. I mean, her body language, the eyes and the way of communicating; it was like, there you go, 'she is the one'!

"You're welcome."

"Anything else, madam?" I continued.

"Come soon," she said and went towards our class.

These two words changed the equation of our bonding at that moment itself. Suddenly she felt closer to me.

It took us twenty minutes to return and bring all the necessities. Amrita, Kamini, and Devesh were holding the decorations and were standing in the passage.

"What happened? Why you guys are standing out here?" I asked.

"Yaar, they are taking too long to clean the room," Devesh said annoyed.

I rushed to the room and saw that very little progress had been made. It was frustrating, so I took the broom and started cleaning the room by myself.

"Give that broom to me," Mansi said.

"It's okay," I said.

She snatched the broom from me.

"You go and manage other things. It will be cleaned in ten minutes," she said.

I saw the same passion in her eyes which I had. It did take ten minutes for the cleaning team to clean the rest of the room as she had said.

It was a ten feet by six feet room. So it hardly took forty-five minutes to decorate the room. We arranged the chairs for the teachers and waited for them to come.

In the meantime, we were relaxing and rehearsing for the function.

"What will you be performing today?" I asked Mansi, knowing she shies from performing.

"I don't sing," she said.

"Then you can dance," I said.

"No, I am a terrible dancer," she said.

"Nobody is a perfect dancer here. I also dance, but I am not a dancer," I said.

"Oh, you dance? Then why don't you dance?"

"No, no, no, don't put this on me. I mean, you could do a *nagin* dance *barati* style," I said.

"No I can't," she said laughing.

"You know nagin dance?" she asked.

"Everybody knows nagin dance, you just have to go through the music and move your hand like this," I said and show her the hand moves.

"No, although I want to do it, but not today," she said.

"Then sing. Everybody is doing something. You should also perform," I said.

"No, not in front of so many people," she said.

"Okay then, sing now in front of me. No one is noticing," I said.

"Alright, if you will sing today, I will sing for you, but first you must," she said.

"There is nothing special in my singing," I said.

"No, I have heard a lot from other people about your performances in school, but I never got a chance to listen," she said.

"Please sing today na," she requested again.

At the same moment, all the teachers came into our room.

"Nice, you've done a great job here!" Rajesh sir said.

"Thank you sir," we said in unison.

All the teachers took their respective seats. Shubham prepared to anchor the function.

It was the moment of truth. All the hard work we had done till now depended on how the function would start and it was on the shoulders of Shubham at that moment.

I was standing outside the class room as there was very less space left in the room where the function was supposed to be held.

Mansi was standing just beside me. I held Mansi's hand. We both remained in the same position till the function ended.

The function went well and at the end, teachers also performed, much to our surprise.

At the end of everything, Shubham said the function would end with a song from Sudhanshu. It was a shock as I thought I had been forgotten.

Mansi insisted, so just to keep her happy, I performed. I sang the song *'Tumhi dekho na'* from the movie *Kabhi Alvida na Kehna.*

After the function, it was time for us to eat and have fun together. Rajesh sir called me into his office. I thought he would congratulate me for the successful arrangements for the function.

As I was going towards the office, I don't know why, but I handed my plate to Mansi. I could have taken it with me to the office or I could have just put it on the table, but I handed it to her.

"We are getting late. How much time will it take you guys to finish?" sir asked.

"Sir, we have to sit and relax and eat the snacks. So it will take around half an hour," I said.

"Okay, but we have to go now. I am giving you the keys. It's your responsibility to lock the rooms after you guys finish," Rishikesh sir said.

The moment he gave me the keys, I knew we now could celebrate freely.

"Ok sir," I said.

They handed me the keys. I went to the room and gave the good news to others. Everybody erupted in joy and started to make noise. There was a lot of glitter left after the decoration, so everybody started to throw glitter at each other. Everyone was running all over the place, screaming and giggling.

Mansi came from behind and rubbed glitter on my face. It was done so neatly that I was not able to notice it. It surprised me. I ran towards her. She ran towards the last room where we had just celebrated the function. It was dark and quiet.

She hid herself behind the door. I noticed her hiding there. So I went there very silently so that she would not notice me. Suddenly I came in front of her; she was not able to move. I took a handful of glitter in my hand.

As I moved my hand towards her neck to rub the handful of glitter on her, she moved her neck upwards towards me as though she had submitted herself to me.

It felt so hot for me that instead of rubbing glitter on her face, I kissed her on her neck. It was a reflex action done in response to her submissive pose. I forgot where I was and who I was and I continued kissing her on her neck, and then kissed her on the cheek.

That's when I heard the other students shouting, playing with glitter. I immediately got away from her as I had got my senses back.

Mansi was still standing there with her eyes closed, not moving her body.

I realized what I was doing was unethical. Because I was in a relationship with Shikha at that time and Mansi had no idea about it. So it meant that I was doing 'wrong' with both of them.

Conversation with Mansi

THE NEXT DAY, WHEN I ENTERED THE CLASS, I SAW Mansi sitting on her seat. I saw her and felt awkward, so I turned my face to the other side and directly went to my seat. She turned backward towards me and looked at me. I looked at her for a few seconds and turned my face away again. I began chatting with Sameer. She noticed the change in my behaviour, but didn't say anything at that moment.

As the classes got over for the day, she came to me. I was standing in the coaching premises talking to everyone about the function. She gestured to me to come with her to a quiet place, but I gestured to her that I was getting late by showing her the watch on my hand and started to walk towards the parking area. She held my hand and like a small baby I went with her.

"Hi," she said.

I looked at her and blinked my eyes in reply.

"Where are you going in a hurry?" she asked.

"I am going home," I said.

"Are you okay?"

"Yeah, I am alright," I said and looked away.

"Hmm…" she said.

I thought this was the right moment to tell her everything and also tell her that what had happened between us was wrong and not ethical.

"Listen Mansi, whatever happened yesterday was a mistake," I said, looking right into her eyes.

"What do you mean?" she said and adjusted her dupatta on her right shoulder.

"Actually, I am in a relationship with someone."

"Oh my god, that's why you stopped yesterday," she said.

"Yeah exactly, that's why I restrained myself," I said.

She paused for a few seconds.

"But all this time you were approaching me… I thought that you like me," she said.

"Yeah, sort of," I said.

"What does that even mean?" she asked and looked annoyed.

"Listen, I like your company. I like it when you are around me. You are a superb girl and if I would not have been with another girl, then I…" I said.

"Who is the girl?" she asked calmly.

"Shikha, she is in my section," I said.

"You love her?" she asked.

"Yeah, I love her," I said.

"Are you happy?" she asked.

"Yeah, I am," I said.

She paused for a few seconds, and this time, she had closed her eyes.

"Listen, I like you and if you think that you are happy with her, then I will never come between your happiness," she said.

"Hmm…," I said.

"But it does not mean that I will stop liking you," she said with a heavy voice.

I looked at her. She was standing calmly, but I could see the grief on her face. I felt that I had done something terribly wrong.

"You are free, Mansi," I said.

"It's my decision to like you or not. It does not matter to me whether you are with me or not," she said.

"But Mansi…"

"Don't say anything," she said.

"Hmm…" I said, burying my gaze at her feet.

"One more thing, promise me that you will interact with me in exactly the same way as before. I just want you to remain the same so that I don't feel that I can't have you in my life," she said as a drop of tear fell down her face.

It was getting difficult for me. For the first time in my life, I had no words to cure her pain. The only thing I could do was console her. So I held her hand in my hand.

"Okay, I promise you," I said.

"I will try to think that we never had this chat so that I will remain in my dream and be happy," she said.

"Don't say that. See, the thing is, I like you. You are a beautiful girl, but you know…" I said.

"I understand," she said. "Can I ask you a question?" she added.

"Yeah," I said.

"If she would not have been in your life, then do you think that our relationship would have been as pure as the one you have with her now?" she asked.

"Right now, it does not matter," I said.

"Hmm…," she said.

She turned her face away. I knew I had broken her heart and now it was my responsibility to get her out of that situation.

"Mansi, nothing has changed. We will be like before," I said.

"I know. Okay, I am going," she said.

She went inside the classroom, took her bag and went out of the coaching premises.

It was comforting for me at some level as I had stopped this as this could have ended in a worse manner. At the same time, I was really worried about Mansi and I promised myself that I would cheer her up, no matter what it took.

But I was wrong, as it's very hard to like someone, and even harder to forget them.

Cricket Match with the Bihar Board

THE RIVALRY BETWEEN THE BIHAR BOARD AND CBSE was started by our super seniors at the coaching centre to find a better group of students each year. And it was not only judged academically, but also by the cricket matches played between both the teams throughout the year. The winning team was given the trophy each year and a special lunch was arranged for them.

These matches were played to balance the fierce and fighting nature of the students in and out of the field. This time it was scheduled for the coming Sunday – 23rd September 2007.

We were representing the CBSE board this year, along with other tenth class and eighth class students. My elder brother was captaining the side and it was solely his responsibility to take us home this time. So he picked the best team available.

Since it was one of the biggest events in our coaching centre, all the students, along with teachers of both the boards, were also invited. More importantly, for me, Mansi was going to be present and watching me play cricket for the first time. So I had to put an impressive performance.

The match was scheduled to take place at the Hawai field. It is the biggest playing ground in Dumra. It is not just a playing ground, but locals used to come to relax and have picnics with their families and spend some quality time together.

The match was of fifteen overs for each side and one teacher from each side would umpire the match. We decided to have the rule of no extra runs. It meant there would be no run given on wide ball, no ball, leg bye or byes. It was the rule we made to save our asses from them because it was our weakness.

The opponent team had some serious players who were tall and pure desi kind of guys. Each one of them was way older than us and was a good athlete. They had beaten us a few times and we had won just once against them, but I was not the member of that team. So it was very important for me to perform well and win this particular match.

It was eleven; time for the toss. We got the news that they had won the toss and we were bowling first. We started to gear up for fielding.

The first over was being bowled by Ketan. He was a senior guy from the tenth class, a diehard fan of Yuvraj Singh; he also looked a bit like him. He was a left hander pace bowler. They had sent two of their best hitters whom I have seen playing previously.

The first ball he bowled was an over pitch delivery and the batsman cleared his front leg and heaved it over the mid wicket for a six. The Bihar board students started jumping in their seats.

It was the matter of a second as I knew they would go after every ball. The next two balls he hit for boundaries and the last ball for a six. So after the completion of the first over, they had scored twenty runs. We were on the back foot in the very first over of the match.

For the second over, Aniket, another tenth class student came to bowl. Another short guy with the specification of a right hand medium pacer. He pitched a short delivery and the batsman on strike pulled it for a huge six. He was hammered for fourteen runs in the over and the score now had become 34 runs after 2 overs without a wicket.

Ketan was again called by my brother to bowl the third over. He was smashed again for three fours in a row, couple of two runs and a six on the last delivery. It was fierce and fearless striking from them. The score had become 56 after 3 overs.

Aniket came to bowl the fourth over and his second over of the match. This again proved to be a better over for them. They scored nineteen runs, including a six on the last ball of the over.

They had put us on a different track now. They were snatching the game away from us and we really needed to take wickets and control the flow of runs. The score was 75 runs for the loss of no wicket after 4 overs.

I asked my brother to give me the opportunity to bowl the next over. Usually I am a pace bowler but at that point, the important thing to do was to not give pace on the ball as they were utilizing the pace provided by our bowlers. So I thought to mix up the slow deliveries with paced ones along with yorkers.

The first ball I bowled was a yorker on the leg of the right hand batsman in front of me. It took the lower outside edge of the bat and went for four through third man region. The crowd started to cheer again for their team.

The second ball I bowled was an off cutter. The batsman tried to heave it through the leg side; it took the edge of his bat and went high and my brother took the catch behind the wicket. A huge cheer was made by our crowd and we were finally happy to get the first wicket.

The batsman had crossed the pitch so it was now the second opener on the strike. The third ball I bowled was a leg cutter, it was pitched on the middle stump and ended up on generating the genuine edge of the bat and my brother took the catch. We erupted in joy as we had sent both the openers back to the hut and now we could have a breather in the match. The next three deliveries I bowled were dot balls. Now the score was 79/ 2 after the completion of 5 overs.

We still had plenty of things on our plate to get right. So I asked my brother to give the ball to those guys who bowl slow. Now our game plan was to restrict them from making runs, and as the pressure of scoring would rise, they would lose wickets eventually.

The next over was being bowled by Devesh. He was much slower than the spin bowlers. He squeezed the over for four runs and the score was now 83/ 2 after 6 overs.

I came in with my second over to bowl. The first ball I bowled with full pace on the off stump line, batsman tried to cut it through the point, but missed it completely. The second ball I bowled with the same line and length, but this time I rolled my fingers on the ball to execute the leg cutter. The batsman tried to put the same shot, but mistimed it and the ball went directly into the hands of the short cover. This was the third wicket for me in the match. I succeeded in stopping a boundary in the over. The score was now 88/ 3 after 7 overs.

Devesh came in with his second over. On the fifth ball of his over, the batsman hit the ball at the point region. Shubham went after the ball, picked the ball and threw it to the bowler's end. It was a direct hit. The batsman was way behind the crease and it was a wicket for us. It was another successful over for us and now the score had became 93/ 4 in 8 overs.

We took the drinks break to plan the strategy for the match. We had to restrict them from making a hundred and fifty runs and for that we had to take wickets at regular intervals. My brother asked me to bowl my last over.

I put all the fielders close to the batsman and no one at the boundary. Everybody thought that it was insane to put the fielders close because a hitter was on strike. He looked at the field and started to wait for me to bowl. I was taking time to make him impatient. I bowled the first ball with full pace on the middle stump. It was a yorker delivery. He tried to heave it through the mid wicket but he missed it and his middle stump went for quite a dance in the air. We started to jump on each other and it was the wicket we had desperately needed. I got another wicket on the fourth ball and it was the only maiden over of the match. Now the score was 93/ 6 in 9 overs.

In the last six overs, they scored another 41 runs and were bowled all out in the last over for 134 runs.

It was an awesome team effort by us to restrict them to this score. We were happy as now the momentum was with us in the match. We needed nine runs per over to score 135 runs in 15 overs to win the match.

We made a strategy to score more runs in the initial overs to put pressure on them and also to release the pressure from the middle order batsmen. So we sent in Niranjan, a tenth standard student and Sameer's brother to the strike. He had gained the reputation of a hitter in our side. I had to go later, so for a brief time, I went to sit with other students of my class to relax and chill with them.

"Nice bowling," Mansi said.

"Thanks," I said.

"Look at them,they all look like married men," Kamini said.

"Hmm… they are much older than us," Amrita said.

"Don't worry, we will handle them," I said.

"When will you go to bat?" Amrita asked.

"Whenever the team wants, and I hope both the openers win the match for us," I said.

Mansi was sitting on the chair. I was relaxing on the ground so she left her chair to sit beside me.

"Drink this," she said.

She gave me a bottle of water.

"It's alright. I just drank a lot of water now," I said.

"Drink, I have brought it for you from home," she said.

"Okay," I said.

I took the bottle and started to drink. It tasted like orange juice.

"What's in it?" I asked.

"It's just juice I made for you," she said.

"Really, you made it?" I said.

"Yeah."

"It's really good. Thanks," I said.

Meanwhile, bhaiya and Niranjan were ready at the middle. Niranjan took the strike for the first ball. He was the Yusuf Pathan of our team. If the ball connects with the bat, it will go the distance, otherwise nothing.

The first ball he tried to heave, he missed completely. The second ball, he connected, and it went over the mid wicket boundary for a massive six. We all started to cheer. A few more shots like that and we'd be at ease with the required run rate. Third ball he defended, it was funny as it was an unexpected block from him. I personally had never seen him blocking the ball. The fourth ball he hit again over the mid wicket boundary for a six. It was the replica of the previous shot. The next two balls went for two singles. Our score was 14 runs after the completion of the first over.

In the second over, my brother was on strike. He took a couple of runs on the first two balls, and then a single, and the fifth ball was shot for the boundary by Niranjan. The score now was 21 runs after 2 overs.

In the third over, bhaiya took a single on the first ball. Niranjan hit the third ball for a boundary after missing the second ball. On the fourth, he lofted the ball, it went very high and he was caught at the boundary. It was the first wicket fallen for us. The next two balls were dot balls. The score now was 26/ 1 after 3 overs.

Prabhat, a tenth class student, came to bat and played the first two balls with soft hands. On the third, he struck down the ground for a single. Bhaiya hit the fourth ball for the boundary towards the cover region and took the single on the last ball of the over before leaving the fifth ball of the over for nothing. The score now was 31/ 1 after 4 overs.

For the fifth over, bhaiya was on strike. He hit the first ball over the mid on reason for six and the next two deliveries, he pulled for two successive boundaries. He took a single on the fourth ball, giving Prabhat strike. He blocked the fifth ball of the over and lofted the last ball. It went straight into the hands of the guy at the long off boundary. It was really unnecessary at that time as it was already a big over. It was really frustrating to see him hitting this unnecessary shot and losing his wicket at this crucial moment in the match. The score now was 47/ 2 wickets after 5 overs.

The sixth over for us went quietly and we only scored five runs out of it, making our score 52/ 2.

In the seventh over, Satya, a tenth class student, was on strike. He missed all the five balls of the over and no runs were scored so pressure was right on us now. On the last ball he was bowled and his off stump went for a walk on the road surrounding the Hawai field. We were again on the back foot. We were 52/ 3 when went out in the middle.

For the eighth over, bhaiya was on the strike to face the first ball. He played the first ball in the air and mistimed it, and was caught out. It was devastating for us and they were jumping all around the ground as they knew the importance of this wicket. Sameer came to take the strike and blocked the first ball. He hit the second ball for a boundary in the cover. The next three deliveries went for two singles. The score now was 58/ 4 in 8 overs. Now we needed another 77 runs in the last 7 overs and we both were the only batsmen left who could score these runs in the overs provided.

I told Sameer that we have to score at least a boundary every over and we should try to rotate our strike to get runs on each ball. It was up to us ninth standard guys in the middle to save our team and board from the loss.

I was on strike for the first ball. I hit the first ball just beside the point region and asked Sameer to run two runs. The next ball, I took a single. Sameer pulled the third ball of the over for the boundary and took a single on the fourth ball. For the fifth ball, I was on strike. I went out of the crease against the fast bowler and hit him over the cover region for six. It felt very nice as it hit the middle of my bat and raised my confidence. On the last ball, I took a single. The score now was 73/ 4 in 9 overs. We still needed 62 runs from the last 6 overs.

I took a single on the first ball of the tenth over. Sameer hit the second ball down the ground and we took two runs, the next ball he defended for no run. He both rotated the strike on the next two balls and Sameer was on strike to face the last ball of the over. He pulled the length ball for another six and it landed where students were sitting. They all started to cheer for us and now they could believe that we were still in the match. The score now was 84/ 4 in 10 overs. We now needed 51 runs in the last 5 overs.

I pulled the first ball of the eleventh over for a six. The next five balls, we scored four singles and took ten runs out of the over. Now we needed another 41 runs from 4 overs.

The next two overs, we scored couple of boundaries and rotated our strike to make 16 runs out of it. So now we needed 29 more runs to win from the remaining 12 balls.

Sameer was on strike to face the first ball of the fourteenth over. He heaved the first ball in the deep mid wicket region for a boundary. He took a single on the next ball. We needed 24 runs from 10 balls. I was on strike to face the third ball of the over. The bowler took the pace off the ball, so I adjusted and went to back foot and swept the ball through the leg side for a six. The next ball he bowled was a bouncer; I tried to hit it, but missed. The next ball he bowled with same line and length and I got on my knees and played the upper cut shot over the head of the keeper for another boundary. I took a single on the last ball of the over. It was a huge over for us and had been desperately needed.

We needed 9 runs from the last over. Everyone was standing on their seats and the crowd that had accumulated to watch this event was making loud noise. It felt like we were playing in a cricket stadium of India.

I was on strike and was under a lot of pressure. The first ball the bowler bowled was on my leg stump, and it hit my bat, then hit my leg and went towards the fine leg region; we took a single. Sameer was on strike now. The next ball, we took a couple of runs. Then the bowler bowled a full toss on the off side of the off stump; he tried to hit with immense power but missed it completely. Now we needed 6 runs from the last 3 deliveries.

Sameer hit the next ball in the deep cover side and we managed to take a double. Four runs needed from the last two deliveries. He hit the fifth ball down the ground to long off region and we ran to take a double, but settled for a single instead.

It was the last ball of the inning, and we needed three runs to win the match. I was on strike and ready to face the last ball. The fielding captain put all his players to the boundary, except the wicket keeper and the bowler. It was a do or die situation for us. I called Sameer and told him if I hit the ball not for the boundary then we had to run three runs anyhow. Don't keep your eyes on the ball and run three, whatever happens.

The bowler started to run for the final time in the match. He bowled the full toss on my leg and I moved towards the off stump and almost sat to hit it over the head of the wicket keeper, it bounced twice and went out of the boundary for four runs.

I remember the first person who jumped on me was Sameer. It was the matter of a second and I was surrounded by all the players of my team. It took me sometime to believe that we had won the match.

Everyone present on the ground were shaking hands and congratulating us, along with the teachers. We were told by Rishikesh sir to follow them to the coaching centre to receive the trophy.

Rishikesh sir and Rajesh sir had arranged lunch for all of us. We ate happily, listening to the praises everyone was showering on us.

I went to Mansi who was sitting on a chair in the back.

"Thanks for the juice, it was really helpful," I said.

"Hmm…" she said and smiled.

You know there are some faces in the world which you see and you almost forget everything around you and it refreshes you; that was the effect of her face and smile at that moment.

"If you want more, I can bring some tomorrow again," she said.

"You should think about it. If it becomes my habit, then you have to bring juice every day," I flirted.

"No problem at all," she said and smiled.

Fight with Aakriti

WE GENERALLY DIDN'T HAVE CLASSES DURING Durga Puja. But this time, we had physics extra classes during vacation.

The thing was that Rumit sir used to fast in those nine days of the puja. So to pass time and to maintain healthy mental strength, he asked us to attend these extra classes. Rumit sir was a dark, short guy, a young man just out of college, teaching students to make his livelihood, with a hairstyle similar to Shahrukh Khan.

Also, it was an opportunity for us to complete our syllabus early, so we agreed to attend the classes. We used to come at noon as by that time he used to complete his morning prayers and rituals.

On this particular day, he decided to take a test. He had brought peanuts with him in his pocket. So he took some of them out of his kurta and told us that they'd be given to those who would give the correct answers. One peanut for each right answer and everybody would have three questions to earn at least one peanut, and those who would not be able to earn even one peanut would have to face punishment.

"Sir, we can do one thing," I said.

"What?" he asked.

"We can give a peanut to the person who has eyes like it," I said.

It was said in the intention of having fun and to lighten the mood before the start of the test. I was in a great mood that day.

Aakriti whispered something and the way she whispered it, I felt that she had said something disgusting about me. I was not sure, but I almost heard some rubbish. I got agitated.

"Whatever a person wants to say, the person should say in front of me, and not whisper like a coward," I said in anger.

"I'll say whatever I want to and about whoever I want to," she shouted.

"But don't act like a coward, have the guts to say it in front of the person," I shouted louder.

I was being patient and polite, and the reason was Mansi.

Mansi turned back towards me and started to look right into my eyes. I could see her eyes, she was worried. Somehow she knew where it was going to end.

Aakriti looked at Mansi, who was still looking at me.

"I have no time to say anything to a person like you," she said.

"Fuck off man!" I said and threw my copy and went out of the class.

It was uncalled for. She had directly made the statement about my personality. It hurt my ego deeply. I took my bicycle and got away from that place as I knew if I stayed there, then I would have done something inappropriate.

Honestly, I felt weak that day because I was not used to hearing these things from the people around me.

This incident changed my attitude in the classes. I stopped talking to Aakriti, Mansi and Kurtika. Mansi tried to come to me and talk with me the next day, but I just remained silent and got away from there. This attitude remained for the next two weeks.

Everybody in the coaching could understand the situation and my anger towards them. So Shubham came to me to talk to me about my recent behaviour.

"Why are you not talking to her?" he asked.

"Whom?" I said innocently.

"You know who I am talking about. You were the only person with whom she used to talk, and now, when she's started to feel better around here, you've stopped talking with her," he said.

"I don't want to talk to any of them. Haven't you heard what her sis told me that day?" I said.

"But *she* didn't said anything na, and after you went out of the class that day, she was really upset with Aakriti," he said.

"But see, she's not trying to initiate any move," I said.

"She must be afraid of how you will react, and listen, I had seen her few times when she had tried to come close to you, but you avoided her and moved away from her each time," he said.

I knew what he was talking about, but I didn't want to admit it at that time.

"The thing is, I want to talk to her, but the moment I see Aakriti with her, I don't know what happens to me. I just stop myself," I said.

"It's all stupidity man! You should talk to her," he said.

"It must be stupidity, but at this moment, I think I am doing the right thing," I said.

"I am telling you that this is not the right thing you are doing. I know you better. You are gonna regret this decision of yours later," he said.

The reality is that I still regret my decision of not talking to her. I wish I could have brushed aside my ego and talked.

"Did you notice no one interrupted you and Aakriti that day?" he said.

"No man," I said.

"Rumit sir could have easily stopped you, but he didn't," he said.

"What is wrong in that, man?" I asked.

"The wrong is that he let you fight because he wanted this to happen. He doesn't like friendship between you and the girls," he said.

"But why?" I asked

"Because I think he likes a girl from our coaching class," he said.

"How do you know this, man?" I said.

"Raghav sir told me. He also told me that Rumit wanted to break your friendship as he used to feel insecure about it," he said.

Raghav sir taught us biology. He was the son of my dad's colleague. He was around twenty-five years old, the same age as Rumit sir.

"Really?" I said in disbelief. "Who could it be? Don't tell me it's Mansi," I said.

"He didn't take any names. Don't worry, it's not Mansi," he said

"How do you know it's not Mansi?" I asked.

"Because, I asked him about her and Aakriti and he said no," he said.

"If Mansi is not in his scope, then why will he let me and Aakriti fight?" I asked.

"May be because you will look bad in front of them!" he said.

"It might be Amrita," I said knowing that Shubham had a soft corner for her.

"Don't say that man," he said.

"I'm just guessing. I hope she is not the one. But, how the hell is he eyeing such a young girl?" I said in anger.

"I asked Raghav sir the same question. He told me that Rumit told him that love is blind."

I laughed my heart out. It was so funny to hear that phrase. Shubham joined me.

"Bro, say one more time 'love is blind'!" I said.

"Love is blind," he said.

It was not getting less funny. The more I used to think about the phrase, the greater the intensity of my laughter became.

Mansi stopped coming to the coaching classes in the third week of November, although Aakriti and Kurtika continued coming.

Rumit sir's birthday

SHUBHAM CAME TO MY HOME AROUND SIX IN THE evening of 15th December. I was sick that day so I was not able to attend the classes. I was walking in the garden. I saw him coming so I walked to the main gate.

"Why didn't you come today?" Shubham asked still sitting on his bicycle.

"I have fever," I said.

"Listen, tomorrow is Rumit sir's birthday and we will be throwing him a surprise party," he said.

He ignored the fact that I was sick and did not even ask how I was feeling.

"Are you mad? How are we gonna prepare for it in such a short time? Also, I am not feeling well. Wait a minute, why do you want to throw him a party anyway?" I bombarded him with these questions.

"Who is throwing the party for him? I am doing this to just spend some time with Amrita. You can ask Mansi to come as well," he said.

I did want to talk to Mansi that someone was spreading rumours about us and it was affecting my relationship with Shikha dismiss all the rumours from her side.

So I agreed. But the problem was where to have it. We couldn't organize it in the coaching centre, not in our houses or in the teacher's. I started to think about these problems and then suddenly Shubham said,

"I know a place."

"Which place?" I asked.

"That I will show you tomorrow. You just wake up early," he said knowing I hated to wake up early in the morning.

"Okay, but don't over think about the party," I said.

I was awakened by Shubham's call at seven the next morning. He asked me to come to road number three. He was waiting outside the gate of one building. I freshened up quickly and cycled to road number three. I saw him outside the gate of an old building. The paint on its walls had faded and looked like one of those old buildings which had been made in the early twentieth century. I saw him and stopped.

"This is the place I was talking about. Meet Amit bhaiya. He is the owner of the house," he said.

I looked at Amit and shook his hand. He was a guy in his late thirties. He was married and was living in Mumbai and used to come once in a year to look after his property in Dumra.

We went inside the house to look around. It was a two storey building. The rooms on the ground floor were relatively small.

We went up to the first floor and there was a big hall filled with antiques. It was a spacious hall where we'd be able to cut the cake and dance.

"How much for the room?" I asked Amit.

"I don't want money. I've already told him about it." He gestured towards Shubham. "You have to bring the diesel so that generators keep running so that you guys don't have any problem.

"Okay, done man," I said.

One more thing, would you like to include me in the party? He asked.

"Bhai, this is the birthday party for the teacher. We all are just students and if you want to come, then you can come at the cake time," I said.

"He told me that girls are also coming to the party." He came close to me and whispered in my ear.

I immediately understood what he exactly meant. Shubham was also there. I saw him with suspicion that what the fuck he meant.

"Arey… what bhaiya? I told you that they are our friends only and again you are asking for these things," he said in anger.

I told Shubham to relax as I was talking to Amit and I would take care of him and asked Shubham to go from here.

"Bhaiya, they are just friends and we are here only to celebrate the birthday party and have fun together," I said.

"But if there is any slack, please include me," he said.

"I assure you that there will not be any such thing happening, and if you still don't have faith on me, then you can be with us to see," I said.

I told Shubham to go to Kamini's house and tell her to call every girl and ask them to come over to celebrate Rumit sir's birthday. And to especially call Mansi to come and tell her that Sudhanshu wanted her to come.

Within half an hour, Kamini, Amrita, and Devesh arrived. I asked Kamini about Mansi. She told me that she'd be coming a little late.

We started to decorate the hall and Shubham went to bring the music system from his house. All the arrangements were coming together well in time. In between, I was going to the balcony attached to the hall to see if Mansi was coming or not.

The news of the celebration spread to the locals when they saw the commotion going on inside and outside the building. It also attracted the attention of the local 'don'. Dumra had a 'don' at each chowk of the city.

Before meeting Shikha I was friendly with all of them, courtesy the cricket matches we used to play with each chowk's team, and it really put me on the wrong track at that time. The moment she came into my life, I left all of them and became a very different guy.

"How are you bhai? You have become the moon of Eid now," Lal Babu, an eighteen-year-old said in excitement, with a smile on his face.

"Arey... how are you bhai?" I said.

I greeted him with a huge smile on my face as it was after a long time I was meeting him.

"Mast bhai, you forget me! Where are you these days?" he asked.

"Na be, you know now I have become nice guy," I said and smiled.

"Arey… bhai, what are you doing here?"

"Nothing be, just throwing a party for the teacher."

"What bhai? I have heard there are girls also in the party," he said.

"They all are friends and really good girls," I said and patted him twice on his shoulder.

"Okay bhai, the owner told me another story, so I came here to see what was happening in my area. But since you are here, I am sure that there will not be any problem," he said.

"You're absolutely right!" I said.

Our preparation was over but there was no sign of Mansi. So we started the celebrations and had a blast in the party and clicked some pics with each other.

Mansi didn't come and Shubham was unable to talk to Amrita as well.

I was really upset at the end, as despite my special invitation, Mansi hadn't come. It made me more vulnerable, as after this, I could hardly have the chance to tell Mansi about the rumours.

The rumours of me involved with her had affected my relationship with Shikha. Although Shikha was not expressing vocally, but I could feel the tension cemented in her mind.

I literally was unable to find any way to convey my thoughts to both Mansi and Shikha.

The talk with Amrita

IT WAS DECEMBER. IT WAS ONE OF THE COLDEST evenings. Only three students had arrived at the coaching centre – me, Devesh and Amrita.

I was having doubts in Sanskrit and asked Rishikesh sir to finish the particular chapter as I had a class test in school the next day.

"It's getting late, you guys should go," Rishikesh sir said.

"It's okay sir. Just finish this chapter as I have a test tomorrow," I insisted.

We finished at around half past seven. The sun had set, and it was quite late, considering the cold weather. Very few people were out at this hour.

"How did you come today?" Rishikesh sir asked Amrita.

"Walking."

"How are you going to go back?" he asked with concern on his face.

"Sir, I can go walking," he said.

"But it's too late. Do you want me to drop you?" he said.

"I can go by myself, sir," she said.

"You go and drop her to her home," he said to me.

"Okay sir, I will drop her," I said.

I left my bicycle in the coaching centre. I could pick it up the next day. We decided to walk. Her home wasn't too far from mine so it was convenient for me to drop her.

As soon as we got out of the campus, we started shivering in the cold.

"It's too cold today," she said and rubbed her hands together to produce some heat.

"Hmm…" I said and blew out some warm air in reply.

"You shouldn't have come. I could have gone alone," she said.

"Yes, you could have, but it's okay," I said.

"I just don't want to be dependent on another person. I mean, I don't require help," she said.

"I know you can, but sometimes it's better to listen to another person," I said.

"You are not getting bored, na?" she asked.

"Oh no. It's a late evening walk," I said.

"Oh yeah." She laughed.

"Whenever anybody asks you whether you are with Shikha, your answer remains no, so if I assume that she is only your friend. Then do you like another girl from our coaching class? I mean do you have crush on anyone?"

"I like everyone here," I said.

"No, I mean is there someone special?" she asked again.

"Since you are here, I will say you," I said.

"No, don't say that."

"No, I am not saying this just because you asked. There is one more reason why," I said.

"What reason?"

"Because I think we are very good friends," I said.

"No, no, tell me what is the reason?" she demanded.

"Listen carefully to what I am saying," I said.

"Okay," she said.

"You know, Shubham bhaiya likes you?" I asked.

"Yes, I know, but…" she said.

"But what, Amrita? He is a great guy. I've known him for a very long time and he always talks about you," I said.

"I know, but I don't feel that way about him. Another thing is that I don't think these things have any kind of future," she said.

"It's because you never give him a chance to explain himself and the other thing is there is no such thing like the future. What you have is the present. Give him a chance and see what happens. If you start liking him, it will be great, and if not, he at least will be happy you tried," I tried to convince her.

"But why?" she asked.

"Because, I, a friend, am telling you to," I said.

She became silent. We were crossing the building in which we had celebrated Rumit sir's birthday.

"You know, we celebrated Rumit sir's birthday here. It was all arranged by Shubham to just spend some time with you. Actually the thing is, we should not bind us in what we like. It's sometimes better to fall in unknown territory also," I said.

She paused for a few seconds. I let her think.

"Okay, I will try," she said after a pause.

"Thank you," I said.

"But he is shy and he doesn't even try that much," she said.

I thought for some time and came up with an idea.

"Okay listen, what are you doing this Christmas day?" I asked.

"Nothing, I will be at home. Why?"

"Do one thing. Go to church with him alone and spend some time together," I suggested.

"Are you sure? He will not say a single word and I know that," she said.

"You should first go and see what he does," I pressed.

"You come along," she said.

"But what I will do in between you guys?" I said.

"Okay, I will ask Kamini to come as well," she said.

I knew if I'd argue further, she might say no.

"Okay, as you wish, but remember, this is for you and him," I said.

"Okay," she said.

We reached her house.

"Thank you for coming with me," she said.

"It's okay, and thank you for listening," I said as she went in.

I was really excited as it was a great news for Shubham. I decided to go to his house the next morning.

Church date for Shubham

I WAS WAITING TO SEE THE REACTION ON HIS FACE
as I had promised him that I'd help him.

I went to his house early around eleven in the morning. I
saw Aunty at the main gate of his house.

"Namaste Aunty, where is bhaiya?" I asked.

"Go to the terrace beta. He is studying there," she said.

I went up on the terrace.

"What are you doing?" I asked.

"I was just going through the history book," he said.

"Why didn't you come yesterday?" I asked.

"It was too cold yesterday," he said.

"Oh okay, I have good news for you," I said.

"What good news?"

"Before that, you have to promise me a samosa treat."

"Tell me the news first," he said.

"Amrita has agreed to listen to you," I said.

The moment he heard that, he jumped up from where he was sitting.

"How?" he asked.

"I asked her to have a talk with you and spend some time together. So I asked her to go church with you on Christmas and she agreed," I said.

"What are you saying?" he said with a huge smile on his face.

"Yeah man! You heard it. The only problem is that she wants me and Kamini to come along," I said.

"It's alright. Now tell me what she said when you told her about me liking her?" he asked pacing up and down in excitement.

"She said she knows it," I said.

"What? She knows? But what will I tell her, then?" he said.

"Whatever you always wanted to say to her," I said.

"God, how?"

"Okay, see the first thing is to act as normal as you can be at that time. And say whatever you want clearly," I said.

"But what is the first thing I will say to her?" he asked.

"Tell her that I want to say something, then tell her that I like you," I said.

"Okay, what else?" he asked.

"You can tell her about the first time you saw her. You can tell her what you can provide her in the relationship. You can discuss these topics with her," I said.

"Oh, I am getting nervous," he said.

He started to move in all directions and I also had to move accordingly to talk with him.

"Everybody gets nervous. You are not the first man to get nervous. Just be yourself and I am sure she will also be as nervous as you are," I said to increase his confidence.

"You think so?" he asked and stopped moving.

"Yes man, I think so. Don't worry. I will also be there," I said.

"Okay," he said.

"Let's go," I said.

"Where?" he asked.

"My samosa is waiting for me," I said.

As planned, Shubham came home around ten in the morning on Christmas day. We were waiting for Amrita and Kamini to call. The plan was that they'd call me when they'd reach near the main gate of my colony. From there we all would go together to the church.

It was a holiday in Sitamarhi. So many people were out on the streets with their family members. It was not common for those people to see four teenagers, specially two boys and two girls, roaming around the city. Everybody was looking at us with suspicious eyes. The fact that we were laughing and shouting also increased their suspicion.

The church on that day looked exceptionally beautiful. We all went inside and could see the pews decorated with fresh flowers; it smelled like heaven there.

We all lit the candles together and made our wishes. I wished that Shikha could get her senses back and stop doing all the 'nonsense' she was doing.

Eventually, we all settled in the open ground just outside the boundary of the church. Very few people were present at that time, mostly couples. It was a nice set-up for Shubham to convey his feelings to Amrita.

I gestured to Shubham to take Amrita away from us. I was left with the 'shop of stupidity', and that is Kamini Priya, and now I had to listen to her. It's amazing how much pain we bear for friends and believe me she was really a pain in the ass.

"Why are they going there?" she asked.

"Oh let them be," I said and tried to ignore her question.

"Amrita told me that you arranged this for Shubham," she said.

"Oh, you know. It's not only for Shubham, it's for Amrita also. Let's see if their friendship progresses to another level or not," I said.

"But I don't think it will happen," she said.

I looked at her and wondered why she was so negative.

"Let them talk. You never know," I said getting annoyed.

"Can I ask you why you are doing this?" she asked.

"It's sometimes better to do some good work for someone else, and both of them happen to be good friends of mine," I said.

However, there was one benefit. Shikha was not responding to me as she used to before. She had started to ignore me and used to make excuses to avoid me. Since she was not listening to me, it became difficult for me to understand this sudden change.

So I started to make things right around me as I was not capable of making things right with Shikha.

"Oh okay… Why do you think Amrita agreed to meet with Shubham here?" she asked.

"Because she has an interest in him and also because I told her to do so," I said.

"She has done this only to keep her word to you," she said.

"Yes, that's what I told you," I said.

"No, there is more. She has a soft corner for you," she said.

"I know that, but the thing is that I can't be with her as I am in a relationship right now, and more importantly, I will never break Shubham's trust," I said.

"Finally, you admit it. It's Shikha right?" she asked.

"Yes, she is the one," I said.

"I knew it. Everybody knew it," she said.

I told her about Shikha only because I thought by telling her about it, Amrita would only focus on Shubham. But it changed everything. Till this date, I regret telling her about me and Shikha, as after this incident everything was going to change for me. It will be clearer for you when you read the section where Shikha takes interest in Vimanshu. That's why telling Kamini about Shikha changed my life.

"Hmm… And believe me, Shubham is the right guy for Amrita. You also know him, so try to convince Amrita to focus on him only," I said.

Shubham and Amrita joined us. We remained seated there for half an hour more and chatted about the weather and other sundry things.

After dropping the girls home, Shubham and I came to my house.

"What did she say?" I asked Shubham.

"Right now, it's thirty-seventy," he said.

"What? Explain in the language which I understand, please," I said.

"I told her that I like her and she replied that she needed some time to think about it," he said.

"Great, give her some time. I think she will agree," I said.

"Okay, thanks man!"

Shikha and Vimanshu

SHIKHA WAS MAKING EXCUSES EACH TIME I USED to approach her. It was almost one month since our last good chat. This was driving me insane.

I had a fight with Shikha over this. I scolded her and asked her to stop doing this. She stopped talking to me immediately and also stopped giving any response.

Two weeks passed and despite all the letters I wrote to her, she didn't respond. She was behaving like a stranger with me and was avoiding me whenever I approached her.

The other day, I went to her and said 'sorry' in front of her friends and told her that I wanted to talk to her. But she refused to talk with me in front of her friends. Her refusal in front of her friends made me mentally weak. I was starting to lose myself.

The next day, I approached her in the lunch break, but again, she refused to talk to me. I still had not lost it completely, so few days later, I asked her to come with me to the field during the classes. At that time she said okay so I moved out of the class, but she never came. I waited for her for around an hour, and when I asked her about it, she gave the lame excuse of being scared of the teachers. I could not believe that because she had done it numerous times before.

One day I saw her looking at one guy in our class. It was Vimanshu, the topper of the class. He was a tall guy with zero sense of humour, and according to me, he was really a duck-faced idiot.

I looked at him and wondered why she was looking at him. I remembered that she had told me that Keshu used to like him. So I thought she must be executing some plan for Keshu so that the duck-faced idiot would come to Keshu and talk to her.

So for the first few days I completely forgot about it. Meanwhile I kept trying to patch up with her and clear her mind about all the bullshit she was hearing about me and Mansi. But every move of mine was going in vain and it was getting frustrating.

One day Keshu was not present in class, but I saw Shikha staring at that bastard. This time I felt that something was very wrong. She remained there for a few minutes and when she noticed that I was looking at her in anger, she got up and went to her seat.

I was not sure what she was trying to do. I was in great confusion. I also thought that she was doing it to make me jealous and vulnerable as she must have been angry about the Mansi thing and also because I would try to talk to her again.

The very next day, she did it again. Keshu was not present in class. This time she looked at me but ignored me and started to stare at that guy. It was clear that she was doing this purposely.

It was devastating for me to see her looking at that bastard in the same manner she used to look at me. I was angry but I was not able to do anything at that moment. As each day passed, it was depressing me.

This interest of hers continued for a long time and she continued avoiding me.

2nd July 2012

Shubham called me as I was packing my luggage.

"Hello," I said.

"What are you doing?" he asked.

"I am packing as I have train tomorrow," I said.

"Did you get admission in PDPU, Gandhinagar?" he asked.

"Yes bhaiya, right now it's an electrical branch. There is every chance of me sliding to the Petroleum branch," I said.

"Congrats. Don't worry, it's a very good college. I heard about the college when I was studying in Vadodra," he said.

"Thanks bhaiya, what about your college?" I said.

"I have applied to a college in Dehradun. I hope I will get admission there," he said.

"All the best brother, I am sure you will get through," I said to raise his confidence.

"Listen, I am sending you a recording of me and Kamini Sinha. I think it will clear your doubts about Shikha," he said.

"It's not required, brother. You know I am over her and I really have no interest to know about her anymore," I said.

"Okay, but I have sent you the recording already," he said.

"Okay bye. I will call you later," I said.

"Bye," he said.

Telephonic conversation between Shubham with Kamini Sinha.

'Can I ask you something?' Shubham asked.

'Hmm... anything,' she said.

'You know Sudhanshu is my best friend and I had always this confusion in my mind about why Shikha was taking interest in Vimanshu back then,' he said.

'Oh that, but why do you want to know?' she asked.

'Just like that ya,' he said.

'Has Sudhanshu told you to ask me this question?' she said.

'Arey... no it's just me asking.'

'I never liked that girl. She is not what she appears to be. There were two reasons for their break-up and the first was Kamini Priya. Actually she came into our class one day with Amrita and she told us that, "there is so much happening between Mansi and Sudhanshu since a very long time. They talk in private and spend time in private. Since Mansi had joined the coaching class, Sudhanshu forgot everything and stopped talking with everybody and only talks with her." The second reason was that Shikha had developed the thought that she could have a much better guy for herself. You remember Kuldeep?' she asked.

'Yeah, the tall guy from our section,' he said.

'She had the same problem with him also. I know Kuldeep since childhood and he had told me everything about her that how mad she is,' she completed.

'Oh my god,' he said.

'Hmm…' she said.

'You know I knew about the Mansi thing, but I never knew the second reason you told me,' he said.

'I told you na. She is a mad girl,' she said.

'Hmm…' he said.

'Where is Sudhanshu nowadays?' she asked.

'He is going to Gujarat to join a college,' he said.

'Okay, tell him that it was better for him that the break-up happened soon. Otherwise it would have hurt him more,' she said.

'Okay,' he said.

'Okay, tell me if there was something between him and Mansi?'

'Yes, they were together, but in the late period of tenth class, and after the break-up between him and Shikha,' he said.

'Hmm…' she said.

This changed everything for me. After such a long time, finally I learnt the truth, and the moment I heard it, a heavy weight was lifted off my heart. Till that day, somewhere I used to blame myself for the break-up.

I also got to know the identity of the person who was spreading rumours about me and Mansi – Kamini and Amrita. Honestly, I could expect this from Kamini because she is a lost cause for me and for her family, but I had never expected it from Amrita.

Bhashan Day Incident

NOTHING WAS GOING WELL BETWEEN ME AND Shikha since the last few months. I had tried to convince her to have faith in me and to continue our conversations, but nothing worked.

There was a lot of tension between us. She was completely brainwashed by 'them' by now. By them, I mean Kamini and Amrita here. Apart from everything I had seen – whether it was her negligence towards me or her taking interest in Vimanshu – I still wanted to try once more to reconcile everything.

It was prep time for our ninth standard final exams. There were no classes for around more than a month for the exams and of one month after the exams. It was already a week and I hadn't had a glance of her. I really wanted to be in touch with her, otherwise whatever chance I had to make things right, would slip through my hand.

So I asked my sister to call her on her only contact number

she had given me. That contact number was her father's cell phone. She dialled the number.

"Hello," Sis said.

There was no reply. She dialled the number again.

"Hello," she said.

No reply. I was getting restless.

"Call again," I said to her.

"I think there is network problem," Sis said.

"Okay, call for the last time," I said.

She dialled the number again.

"Hello," she said.

"Hello," a man said.

But the call got disconnected at this moment. My sis and my mum were going to see the Saraswati idols procession from the main gate of the colony. They were getting late for it.

"Okay, go now, but come soon as I really want to talk to her," I said.

They went to the main gate of the colony to watch the procession with other ladies of the colony. I walked in the compound watching the procession from there.

I saw Shubham Aashu coming towards my house. So I went out to meet him.

"What are you doing here? I saw your mum and sis at the main gate," he said.

"Nothing bhaiya, I am waiting for them," I said.

"What waiting? Let's go, we will also watch the procession," he said.

"But bhaiya, I don't want to go," I said.

"Arey come, it will be fun," he said.

"No bhaiya, I really don't want to go," I said.

"Don't do drama and don't act like 'Devdas'. Let's go, have some fun and fresh air," he said.

"Ok, but let me change," I said.

"No, there is no time for changing anything. Take the keys of the bike; we will go towards Shikha's house also," he said.

My brother was one year senior to me and he was appearing for his tenth board exam that year. He was the only person left in the house that evening.

So I told him that I was also going to see the procession and I was taking the bike with me.

We went to see the procession at Shankar Chowk and towards our coaching centre at Hanuman Chowk. Another aspect of going to the procession was the girls. Every beautiful girl of Dumra used to come out to watch the procession.

Shubham took me there so that I could get my mind off Shikha. But all I could think of was her. I wanted to go home as soon as possible and call her.

"Bhaiya, let's go home," I said.

"Don't you want to go towards her house?" he asked.

"But, I think it will be much more crowded there," I said.

"Don't worry, we can steer through on a bike," he said.

We went towards her house, but it was unceremoniously silent. There was nothing happening. So we took a round of the street where she used to live and returned home. Shubham took his bicycle and went home.

I parked the bike in the front of the veranda and went directly to the hall where my sis was sitting. My elder brother was also there discussing something with her. I sat down. After a few minutes, my brother handed me the mobile phone.

"A call came from this number," he said.

It was Shikha's number. I got a bad feeling right away.

"Ok, you didn't pick up the call?" I asked anxiously.

"No, I picked the call. Some man was asking about you," he said calmly.

I knew the moment he said a man, that the man must be her dad.

"Yes, he asked me who I was," he said.

"What?" I said.

"I told him that we study in R.A.V. school, my name, my class, and your name, your class."

I was looking at my brother with disbelief in my eyes.

"He asked me why I had called. I told him that my brother must have called," he added.

"He asked me about the girl who calls first and asks for Shikha, so I told him that she is my sis. She calls first and then my brother takes the phone from her," he completed.

I was stunned and was looking continuously at my brother with anger, disbelief and anxiety.

"And?" I asked.

"Nothing," he said.

"What did the man say at last?" I asked.

"No, he didn't say anything. He just asked me questions and I answered him."

"But, how could you tell him everything?" I asked.

"What do you mean?" he said.

"You know I love her and called to talk to her," I said.

"I didn't know. You never told me about her," he said.

"I thought that man knows you, that's why he was asking about me as well," he added.

I didn't know what to say to him at that moment. I was angry with him, but it was a blunder he had made unintentionally.

The moment I heard all this, I got into a state of anxiety. I had got her into trouble. All I could think of was her situation at her house.

I decided not to call her again and to call Keshu in the morning and discuss what happened with her.

I kept the mobile phone with me so that I could call Keshu early in the morning and could ask her to talk to Shikha and ask if she was alright or not. I was worried about her as I knew her father was going to make her miserable.

I woke up late in the morning as I barely got any sleep in the night. I saw two missed calls from Shikha at ten in the morning. So I called her back immediately.

"Hello Sudhanshu?" she said.

"Hello, yes!" I said.

"How dare you call me?" she shouted.

"I wanted to talk to you," I said and got out of my bed to stand on hard ground.

"But why did you call me on my phone?" she said.

"I told you I wanted to talk to you," I said calmly.

"What do you think of yourself?" she shouted again.

"Nothing, I just wanted to talk and make things clear," I said.

"But how dare you call on my number?" she repeated.

"How I am supposed to talk to you if I don't call you?" I said.

I could hear voices of other persons whispering. I calmed myself and thought that she must have been told to call in front of them. So she is showing them anger towards me. I was still thinking positively about her; it's what love does.

"You don't dare call me when I am at home," she said.

"But just listen to me once," I said.

"Shut up! Never call on this number. I hate you!" she screamed before hanging up.

When I heard the statement 'I hate you', it got stuck in my mind. I wanted to call her again, but I just could not.

When you are mistreated by the person whom you used to love and care for, it hurts. This incident turned me into a bad person.

I was disgusted with myself at that time. I was thinking that she must have been pressurized by her family members to call me and end everything with me.

I fully blamed myself at that time, and when you are in this situation, where you know she already had doubts about you with another girl, this phone call proved to be a blunder.

I was not able to think straight and it made me more confused. Due to this confusion, I again kept trying to convince her until 'someone' asked me to stop this nonsense.

My Fight with Myself

IT'S GOOD TO BE A HERO, BUT WHEN A HERO becomes a zero, it becomes very hard for him to regain his place. And during this transition period, the biggest fight he has is with himself. The worst thing about it is that you don't know how you've gotten into it and also don't have any idea of how to get out of it.

I am not from another planet, so it happened to me also. It all started when I had a fight with Aakriti. Due to the fight between me and Aakriti, I stopped talking to Mansi. My ego made sure I completely lost any connection with her.

Mansi stopped coming to the coaching class from the third week of November, 2007. Initially I thought that she must be sick, but later in the first week of December, when asked by the teacher in the class, Aakriti said that she was gone for good.

The same day, Vinay came to me and said that I was the reason why she was not coming as I wasn't behaving well. I became angry and abused him in front of other people. I knew somewhere I was doing wrong, but my ego took control of me. Although Vinay didn't leave me immediately, but later he changed his seat and gradually stopped approaching me.

I lost another person who was close to me. In the same first week, Shikha stopped coming to meet me. It was I who used to go to her and then she'd talk. Few days later, I got the sense that she was upset with me because someone was bad-mouthing her and telling lies and spreading rumours about me and Mansi.

This was a wake-up call me for me and I did wake up. I tried my best to keep up with all of them, but they were now in the zone from where there was no coming back.

I went to Vinay and tried to explain things to him, but he never was the same Vinay again who had been my good friend. I tried to talk to Mansi, that too in vain.

I must have tried almost every day to talk with Shikha about the rumours, but she used to ignore me. I always asked her that if she wanted to clear something with me, she could come and ask me, but she never did.

It was tough for me and I am sure it would have been much tougher for her also to listen to the rumours, but if you will not discuss it with your partner, then it will never be solved. All those rumours took over her mind, fuelling her interest in Vimanshu.

She thought that she could do better than me. And when I heard the phone recording between Shubham and Kamini Sinha, it opened my eyes and everything become crystal clear.

Somehow she wanted to break-up with me as the thought of superiority took over her 'little' mind. But it was painful for me.

It is never easy to see your love looking at another guy in the same manner as she used to look at you. The moment you see it, you completely lose yourself. I was blaming myself at that time because I thought that it was the rumours of me being involved with Mansi that were making her do these stupid things.

Sameer was now not the same friend of mine. This was the second hardest thing for me to accept after Shikha's indifference. We were friends since a long time and had done every silly thing together, along with Siddharth. He was now sitting with Vinay in the row in which Vimanshu sat. That guy had taken everything away from me, including my best friend.

The Bhashan day incident was the lowest point in my life at that time. She refused to talk to me on the phone and blamed me for that. I have no shame to admit that I was depressed at that time. I was unable to eat well and everyone in my family was worried about me. I was not able to sleep at night.

All my innocence was gone. I was not the same Sudhanshu who was vibrant, cocky and expressive. He was lost. I was not able to focus on my surroundings.

All my charm was lost and I almost stopped interacting with everyone. Many people asked me 'what happened'. I used to look at them and never reply.

I appeared for my ninth final exams in this state of mind. It reflected in my result as I didn't score well.

It was now the month of April and we were in the tenth standard. I tried for another month to talk to Shikha, but she never responded. After four weeks of trying, I understood that it was over.

I made up my mind to not approach her in my entire life. And soon I started to get over her. But still, my charm and my innocence were lost.

During these tough times, only one person remained with me, and that was Shubham. He was the person who raised my confidence when I needed it the most. He reminded me about all the good things in life. He took care of me like an elder brother and that's why I've always called him 'bhaiya'.

My real recovery started when my cousin came to Sitamarhi and when I went to Kolkata. He gave me the assurance that there are more girls in the world other than her and also suggested to me to try to make another girlfriend. He told me that everyone goes through break-ups. In fact, he said I'd have the chance of meeting new girls now.

The same happened with me when I met Amanda in Kolkata. She proved to be a real angel who came in my life and gave me the sense of real enjoyment. She taught me how to get over my break-up, and that too in a splendid way. I will always have respect and love for her for helping me regain my confidence with girls.

I have no words to explain the influence of Mansi in my life. She was, she is and she will remain the biggest part of my life. She brought back my innocence, my charm, my attitude. She will always remain in my heart and in my mind.

Now, the second innings of this story starts, where I find a way for myself to get away from all the negativity.

Cricket Match in School

IT WAS THE RITUAL FOR BOARD STUDENTS TO PLAY a cricket match to relax amidst the hectic time table of tenth standard in our school.

The match was played between the students of tenth class and the opponent team which included ninth, eighth and seventh standard students.

I always used to captain the side I played for, but this time, I let Sameer be the captain, the reason being that I was in 'that' situation.

It was a bright sunny day and the match was scheduled to start at eleven in the morning. All the teachers, students and the principal were present on the ground and watching us play.

The most important thing was that Shikha and Mansi both were present on the day and were watching the match.

We won the toss and Sameer elected to bat first. Aman and Sameer went for the opening and he asked me to bat at third position. He knew that I always used to open, but since it was his team, I let him have this change.

Sameer took the strike for the first ball. A junior was bowling the first over. He was tall, lean and was long-haired. The first ball he bowled was an over pitch delivery. Sameer lofted the ball over the mid wicket; it bounced once and went past the boundary line.

Every tenth standard student started to cheer. It was a perfect start for us in the match. The second ball was way outside the off stump and was called wide ball.

The next three balls were gone for boundaries. Sameer smashed each delivery towards the leg side for the Jharu Baharu shot. The Jharu Baharu shot is one in which a batsman swings the bat to his natural side. It looks like a sweep shot. The next two balls were length deliveries; Sameer tried to hit them with full power, but missed both.

So at the end of the first over, we were at 17 for the loss of no wicket. It was a great start for us as it was a huge over.

In the second over, Aman was on strike for the first time in the match. He was a destructive batsman. The second over was being bowled by Ankit, a ninth class student.

He bowled the first ball which was patiently left by Aman as it was on the off stump line with sheer bounce and good pace. The second ball was a short pitch delivery in the line of the body. So Aman pulled it; it took the edge of the bat and went very high and he was caught out at short mid wicket. Juniors started to cheer.

So now the score was 17/ 1. It was my turn now, so I took my bat and went to the crease. Sameer came to me and told me to give him the strike as much as possible as he would be hitting the shots. If he got out, at least I'd be there to score runs.

The first ball I played was a full toss, so I played it with a straight bat to the long on for a single. For the fourth ball, Sameer tried to heave it over the head of the bowler, but it took the edge of the bat and remained in the air for some time before dropping at point region. He wanted to run, but I stopped him.

I went to him and told him to relax as we were good with the run rate and suggested to him to first see the ball, then hit the ball. The fifth ball he hit over the head of the bowler for boundary, but this time, he saw the ball till he hit it with his bat.

On the last ball, he took a single to retain his strike in the next over by playing it gently in the cover area. We were 23/ 1 after 2 overs.

To bowl the third over a spinner came to ball. Sameer was a hitter so it was really difficult for him to hit the spinning ball. The first ball of the third over was an off spin ball. It was dropped at the fifth stump and it ended hitting his leg, right in front of his leg stump. He looked at me with surprise.

He came to me and asked me whether he should continue hitting in this over or not. I suggested him to stay on the crease and try to hit the ball gently as there were plenty of overs left in the match; we could score later. So for all the next five deliveries, Sameer stayed there and didn't try to hit it. It was a maiden over.

To bowl the fourth over, Ankit came. I was on strike. The first ball was a bouncer. But it didn't bounce as much as expected and ended up hitting me on my head. It was painful. Ankit came to me and immediately said sorry. Umpires signalled a break and called for a pain relief spray.

In between the break, I accidently looked towards Shikha and she was talking to someone, but when she saw that I was looking at her, she turned her face to the other side immediately.

It raised my anger and now I was not feeling the pain as it was replaced by the pain she was causing. I told the umpire that I was ready and I was going to continue batting.

So the match started again, only this time I was focusing more than before on hitting the ball.

The second ball he bowled was again on the same line, but this time, I quickly went on the back foot and pulled it with all the power I had for a boundary. It went like a bullet the moment it hit my bat. There erupted a huge cheer in the crowd. Sameer came to me.

"Nice shot," he said.

The third ball was again on the same line, but on the fourth stump now; so I made room and hit it past the point region for another boundary. Sameer smiled as he knew I was now in my zone of batting and he knew what could happen in the match now.

The fourth ball was a low full toss. I drove the ball straight past the bowler and it went for a four again. It was timed to perfection by me. The cheer made by the crowd was unstoppable now as they were watching the vintage me. They started to chant my name. Now the score of our team was 35/ 1.

The fifth ball was a slow one. So I moved towards the off stump and hit it with immense power. The ball went out of the school boundary for a six. One of the umpires who was our teacher came to me and asked me to take it easy.

I smiled at him. The ball was not found, so the umpire called for a new ball.

When the match restarted, the sixth ball was an over pitch delivery, so I heaved it with full power and it went very high. It looked like it would cross the boundary, but it stopped in the air and started to fall. Someone took the catch. The juniors started to cheer for their team again.

So our score was now 41/ 2 after 4 overs. I was upset with myself as I really wanted to score more runs.

Now it all depended on Sameer to score runs. But after I got out, he became nervous and started to play defensively. It started to affect our run rate and the other batsmen in our team did nothing. They were getting out one by one, playing shots in the air.

From being at 41/ 2 in 4 overs, we were all out at 56 in 8 overs. It was not a big score, but we had faith that we could stop the juniors from meeting the target.

So we geared up to stop them from making these 56 runs in 12 overs. The first over was bowled by Sameer. He was enjoying all the benefits of being the captain.

He gave five runs in the first over. I asked him to give the ball to me as I thought that the only way we could restrict them was by taking wickets at regular intervals, and it was the start of the innings for them. I wanted to take one wicket and put pressure on them.

I bowled the first delivery and it went leg side for a wide. I bowled the second ball and it was again called wide as it went outside the leg stump.

The culprit was my full sleeved shirt. I used to wear it just for the feel good factor and also to cover my broken right hand.

Due to the shirt, I was not able to swing my hand properly, and due to this, the ball was ending at different angles. I bowled eight wide balls continuously, and with each wide ball I bowled, the juniors were making more noise. It was eventually making me more nervous. Sameer asked me to go for the baby over, but I said no to him. I removed my shirt in the middle of the ground and bowled in the round necked black-coloured t-shirt I used to wear inside.

I completed the over and also took a wicket on the last ball. The score card was 15/ 1 in 2 overs.

We fought back hard in the next overs and restricted them from scoring boundaries with wonderful fielding.

They needed seven runs from the last two overs. For the second last over, Sameer came to bowl. He conceded only four runs. Now they required three runs from the last six balls. Sameer asked me to bowl the last over, but I refused.

My refusal to bowl the last over was new for him. He knew that I was not able to focus on the match. But I refused him due lack of confidence in me.

Aman went to bowl the last over and eventually we lost the match. My refusal didn't go well with Sameer. He thought I refused because I didn't want the team to win the match under his captaincy. Like Vinay, he must have thought I had done him wrong. I think this was the day which proved to put the final feud between our friendship and he completely stopped approaching me.

First Step to Recovery

IT WAS THE SUMMER OF 2008. WE HAD A VACATION of a month and a half. My uncle, who used to live in Kolkata, had come to Sitamarhi to visit us with his son, Nicky bhaiya. My uncle is my father's elder brother and is third in terms of age among five brothers.

I discussed the recent turmoil in my love life with Nicky bhaiya. I told him everything. As an elder brother, he advised me to come with them to Kolkata this vacation to keep my mind off Shikha.

My parent also advised me to go and have fun as they were still worried about me. They told me to stay there as long as I wanted to. So the tickets were booked.

This was the first time I was travelling such a long distance. Although I have been to Kolkata before, but at that time, I was only two years old and I had no memory of it. There is one story related to that trip which my mother often tells me.

Actually when I was just two years old, I got lost in the market just outside the Howrah station in 1995. My mother is not different from other Indian mothers. She started crying as she was not getting any clue of me. My father and my uncle started to look for me in the market around the station, but there was no sign of me. At last, when they were going to report for the lost children in the railway police office, they saw me in the lap of a lady who was selling flowers. I saw my mother and father and started to cry loudly. My mom heard my cry and went to that lady and snatched me from her hands. The lady got angry and started to shout why you are taking this baby; this one is mine. My mom got angry and started to curse her. It grabbed the attention of people and they started to accumulate there. My father asked the flower lady how much money she wants for me as it was clear she was not making easy for them to get their child back. At the end, my father gave her some money and then the matter was closed.

We arrived at Patna bus stand at noon. Now we had to wait for our train as it was in the evening on the same day.

As planned beforehand, we went to a hotel and booked a double bed room so that we could relax and get fresh before the start of our journey in the night for Kolkata.

We left the hotel around half past four in the evening, and went to the station. It was the Rajdhani Express by which we were to travel. The train arrived at the station at the right time and we settled in our berths. I got the side lower birth. In the night, I was not able to sleep, so I drew aside the curtain of the window and started to look outside. The train was running very fast, I could hardly see anything.

Soon the memory of Shikha started to flow in my mind, and with the memory, the anxiety returned. I started to sweat heavily despite the A.C. compartment. I got out off my berth to go outside the compartment to get some fresh air.

As I opened the door, I saw a girl in her early twenties standing in front of the mirror and looking at her face. As I opened the door of the compartment to step out, a gush of wind flowed in. I stood there with my eyes closed for at least five minutes.

As I opened my eyes, the girl was still standing in front of the mirror.

This time I noticed her; she was wearing a jeans and a top and at least four inches high-heeled sandals. I started to conjure stories about her in my mind as each one of us does when we see strangers. She turned towards me and saw me looking at her.

"What happened?" she asked.

"I wanted to ask you why you are continuously looking at the mirror," I said.

She looked at me up and down and moved towards the door to stand in front of me. A lovely feminine smell took over my senses.

I was wearing a black t-shirt and jeans and had a 'Hanumani' around my neck. Well, a Hanumani is a piece of gold made in the shape of lord Hanuman and it is tied around the neck with a red thread.

I think every Bihari child must be aware of it.

"You were looking at me," she said.

"Yeah I saw you staring at the mirror so I was wondering what is wrong with you," I said.

"I was looking at my face," she said with smile.

"Why?" I asked with confusion on my face.

"To see how beautiful I am," she said and did something cute with her eyes.

She was really beautiful, but the way she said it showed her confidence. She was proud of herself. She knew it and nothing in this world could shake her from thinking so.

It was an eye opening statement for me. It changed my thought process. You should be confident of yourself, otherwise there is no point of the existence of life.

"Thank you," I said.

"For what?" she asked.

"You are really beautiful," I said.

"Thanks but…" she said.

I locked the door and went back to the compartment. Soon after, I went to sleep.

I was awakened by the waiter serving the morning tea.

My uncle and my brother were also awakened by the chaos created by the waiters of the Rajdhani Express. I was joined by my brother who was on the upper berth. Our train was scheduled to reach Kolkata in half an hour. This was my first train journey which was going to be completed at the scheduled time.

We reached Kolkata at ten past six. I took my bag and went out of the train. The moment I got out of the train, I found myself in the middle of thousands of people disembarking.

The Howrah station is a massive one and I never had seen such a big railway station before. The roof top seemed to be as high as a five-storey building.

We took the famous yellow taxi. My brother was giving me a tour of the city as we were crossing the Howrah Bridge.

In the morning, Kolkata looks like a laidback city. People do their work as they have enough time in their hand. The smells of flowers and fish blown by the fresh air coming over from the Hugli River were quite overwhelming.

We reach home after a fifty-minute drive from the station. My aunty, another brother and sister were waiting for me. We were meeting after a very long period of time and we all were excited to see each other.

That day in the evening, we played short pitch cricket in the street of the colony. I saw an extremely fair girl with blonde hair standing in the balcony of her house, looking at us. She was wearing a blue top and a white short skirt. The sunlight made her blue eyes shine more. Her pink lips were attracting my eyes.

Her house was in the direction in which I was fielding. I was looking at her continuously. She looked at me and she noticed it. She started to stare at me, and when I didn't take my eyes off her, she looked away; after a few seconds, she again looked at me for a moment and went inside her house

"Bhaiya, who was she?" I asked my brother.

"Who?"

"That girl, who was in the balcony now," I said.

He looked at me and smiled.

"She is from the UK. She is staying with Subhash uncle and their family as she is the daughter of his business partner in UK. They are a very rich family."

"Why? What happened? She is beautiful, right?" he added.

"Yeah, she is really pretty," I said and smiled.

The very next day, my aunt told me to get ready as we were invited by Subhash uncle's wife for lunch at her house. I became excited as I'd get a chance to see the English girl. I put on my best t-shirt and got ready.

They had a beautiful house. We went inside the house and it felt like I was on the sets of a daily soap. It was designed to perfection.

My aunt introduced me to the lady of the house, her two daughters and the English girl. She told me that their daughters were studying in college in the same year and also introduced the other girl as a family friend. Her name was Amanda and she was also in college back home.

We sat at the dining table. It was my first proper Bengali feast. I was trying all the dishes for the first time in my life. They introduced me to some of the dishes and also gave me a brief history about it. Most of the dishes I tasted were sweet and they told me that Bengali food is usually sweet because they like to enjoy and celebrate their food and sweetness gives you rush of being high. It also makes you feel that you are celebrating each time you have a meal.

She also told me that she and my aunt are best friends and whenever they get a chance, they spend time with each other. It was really making sense to me as they really were behaving like long lost sisters.

After lunch, my sis asked me to join her and the other girls at their terrace garden. Again the terrace garden was something which I was seeing for the first time in my life. We settled on the floor of the terrace.

"What do you do?" Palomi (elder daughter of Subhash uncle) asked.

"I am in school studying in the tenth standard," I said.

"How old are you?" she asked.

"Fifteen and a half; I will turn sixteen this September," I said.

"I like your hair," Mimi (younger daughter of Subhash uncle) said.

My hair has been a great asset and I always take special care.

"Thanks," I said.

"What? You know it's rude to not to compliment to the person who pays you a compliment," she said and adjusted her hair.

I looked at her. This was new for me. It was my first exposure to Bengali girls and my first experience was telling me that they liked to chit-chat and also liked to talk about themselves.

"Oh, you are also beautiful," I said.

"Too late, but anyway, why do you think I look beautiful?" she said with a smile.

"I mean, you have a beautiful face and eyes," I said.

"She is just pulling your leg, bhai. She is like this," Sis said.

"Oh, no. I am good. What's your name?" I asked the foreign girl.

"Me? Amanda," she said as she was not expecting my sudden interest in her.

"Bhai, aunty just told you her name," Sis said.

This was the first time I was interacting with any foreigner.

"This is the first time I am speaking to a foreigner and my English is not so good," I said.

"Okay, but I can understand you," she said with a smile.

"I like your smile," I said looking right into her eyes.

"Thanks," she said and adjusted her hair.

"Wow bhai, you started to make your move," Sis said.

I looked at Amanda; she was smiling. I had never seen that kind of elegance in other girls in my life. It was just beautiful to watch her talk, her hand movements and the gestures she was making. I could have looked at her all my life if she would have agreed to sit in that position.

I realized I was completely into her and I really wanted to get to know her better.

The same evening, as we were playing cricket in the street, she came out to her balcony and was enjoying the sunset. I saw her. She saw me. And this time, she didn't take her eyes off me. Each time I looked at her, she was looking at me. This staring game continued for the next few days until one day she along with Palomi and Mimi came to our house one afternoon.

"Bhai, get ready, I will give you a tour of the city," Sis said.

"Okay, but it's too hot outside," I said.

It was a really hot and humid day. I was sweating like a pig indoors, and was wondering how harassing it's going to be out there on the streets of Kolkata.

"Bhai, it's not a problem. We will go take the metro; it's air conditioned," she said.

"Really, but what about the streets?" I said.

"What bhai, Amanda is also coming with us. Come join us," she said.

"What? You should have told me. Let's go," I said.

I got ready within five minutes and went out to the living room. Amanda was looking stunningly beautiful. She was wearing a top and denims with sneakers. I thought how in the hell I will be able to make moves on such a beautiful girl. Clearly she was out of my league, but I thought at least I could try once and see what happens.

We went to see the Victoria Memorial first. My sis told me that it was made for the princess at that time. It was really overwhelming to see such a historic monument. I was really keen to impress Amanda, so I walked with her.

"It's astonishing," I said and gestured towards the palace.

"Yeah, it is."

"But not more than you," I said looking towards her.

"Thanks," she said and looked at me.

"Are you single?" I asked.

"I broke up with my boyfriend before coming here."

"Oh sorry!" I said.

"It's alright, and you? Are you single?"

"Sort of!" I said.

"What does that even mean?" she asked.

I narrated the events in brief.

"…And the funny thing is we still have not officially ended it," I continued.

"Oh, you poor thing!"

"I am here to recover from it," I said.

"That's great. You know, I am here for the same thing," she said.

"Then we can help each other getting out of it," I said and smiled.

I looked at her but she seemed to be mentally elsewhere. So I didn't try to force my point of view on her.

We returned home and I got ready to play cricket. I was eagerly waiting for Amanda to come out to her balcony. If she would come out, then it meant she had taken my last statement positively, otherwise it was going to be end of me having any chance with her.

After twenty minutes or so, she came out to her balcony. I looked at her and waved at her and she did the same with a huge smile on her face. I knew that moment that I had succeeded with the first hurdle.

Now I was searching for some quiet time with her. I got the opportunity very soon.

Two days later, I was lying on the bed and was watching the IPL match between Chennai Super Kings and Kolkata Knight Riders. It was the third match of Kolkata and I was excited as in the very first match, Brendon had scored more than a hundred and fifty runs. But I was the supporter of the Chennai team as Dhoni was captaining the team. Kolkata had won the toss and elected to bat first. So it was important to watch Brendon again.

My aunt came to me, gave me a bag and asked me to give it to Subhash uncle. I jumped out of my bed in excitement, got fresh and took the bag and went to his house.

I rang the bell and waited eagerly to see if Amanda would open the door. The door opened and it was aunty.

"Hello aunty, my aunt sent this bag," I said and I raised my hand in which the bag was.

"Oh yes, come inside beta," she said.

I went inside and she asked me to sit in the living room as I handed the bag to her. She took the bag and went inside. I was looking in all directions for Amanda in that big house, but she was nowhere in sight.

I saw aunty coming out of the room and going to the kitchen.

"Aa… aunty where is Amanda?" I asked.

"She must be on the terrace, beta. Go up. I am bringing some snacks for all of us," she said.

"Okay aunty," I said.

I rushed to the terrace and looked for her everywhere, but she was not there. So I went to her room. She was watching something on her laptop. She was wearing a green dress and looked lovely. I stood right beside the table.

"Hi. You are here," I said.

"Hi. Yeah, why?"

"I was looking for you all over the terrace as aunty told me that you will be on the terrace," I said.

"Yeah, I usually go there," she said.

"What are you watching?" I asked.

"It's a video on YouTube."

"Can I say something?" I said.

"Yes please," she said.

"I like the way you talk. I mean, I like your elegance," I said looking into her eyes.

"Thanks."

"Can I kiss you?" I asked.

She looked at me and smiled. She came near to me and she kissed me on my lips for a moment and moved back. That touch of her lips felt very smooth. It was more than enough to ignite my willingness to kiss her back. So I moved forward and took her in my arms and kissed her. I could taste the strawberry lip gloss. I had already thought to go beyond the kiss. So I moved my hand in her silky hair and held her by her neck, bent her and kissed multiple times on her neck. I could smell the odor of her body and it was tempting me to have her more and go further.

I was not me at that time. I was lost somewhere in her beauty and in the excitement to have her in my arms under my control. The comforting thing was that she was not standing like a dead fish, but was responding with the same excitement and passion.

I turned her to the other side and kissed her on the nape of her neck. I could feel her breathing; it was getting out of her control. I bent her on the table, pulled the chain of her one piece dress down and kissed multiple times on her back.

I looked at her and thought I should ask her what went wrong in her relationship.

"Don't you want to tell me about your break-up?" I said.

"It's not entertaining like yours. It was a simple relationship. That's it," she said.

"Can I ask you a question?" I said.

"Yeah!" she said.

"How old are you?" I said with a smile.

"Seventeen!" she said.

"Wow. You know you are an awesome girl and I will tell my grandchildren about you," I said.

She smiled.

We spent time together at every opportunity we could get and it really helped me getting my mind off Shikha and from the side effects of the break-up with her.

After staying there for three more weeks, it was time to say goodbye to everybody, especially Amanda. So before leaving Kolkata, I went to talk to her.

"I'm leaving tomorrow," I said.

"Yeah, I remember. What time is the train?" she asked.

"It's at two in the afternoon, so I'll be leaving home at twelve," I said.

"Ohkay!" she said.

I looked into her eyes. She was not showing any emotion, but I knew that she was sad.

"What's next?" she asked.

"I don't know if I will be able to develop any sort of healthy relationship with other girls," I said.

"Don't say that. You are an amazing lad and I am sure you will find a beautiful Indian girl for yourself," she said.

"You think so?" I said.

"Yeah, I think so!"

"Thank you for making my journey exciting and I will cherish and remember the memories with you for life," I said.

"No. I should say thank you. You are a great guy and always be like that. Don't lose yourself, whatever happens," she said.

"Yeah, I will and you too," I said.

She came forward and hugged me. I kissed her on her forehead and on the cheeks and at last on her lips. We chatted for a while before saying goodbye.

My brother came to drop me at the Howrah station. I said goodbye to my brother and the train left the Howrah station.

I remember I was saying god bless Kolkata sitting in the train as it had really proved to be a turning point of my life. I have been to Kolkata numerous times after it and whenever I land here, it still gives me goose bumps and it will remain in my heart till my last heartbeat.

Fight with Vimanshu

I USED TO SIT WITH SHUBHAM IN THE TENTH CLASS. Sameer and Vinay used to sit just behind my bench in the ninth standard. But they had changed their seats and went to sit with Kuldeep, Vimanshu, and Prakash.

Kuldeep was the guy who proposed to Shikha way before I even knew she existed. Prakash was his best friend. I never got along with them, although he never came to discuss this incident with me and take out his frustration.

Shikha had told me earlier about Kuldeep and she also told me that he was a psycho kind of guy who had proposed to her numerous times even after she rejected him each time.

Vinay was not talking to me due to Mansi. He thought I was the reason why Mansi never took interest in him. I don't blame Vinay completely for thinking like this, but he also never ever approached her.

Sameer and Vinay were better friends now than before. Vinay was a rich guy who used to have a lot of pocket money, way more than I used to get.

Sameer knew about Vinay. Now he could have access to the money. So I was not required now.

They put the boundary between our friendship. They stopped talking with me around the start of the tenth class.

I tried numerous times to start connecting afresh with both of them, but it was hurtful as they used to ignore me.

It was the last period and I was looking at Shikha staring at Vimanshu.

"What are you looking at?" Sameer said.

"You know everything," I said.

"Whatever he is looking at, he is not getting," Vimanshu whispered.

I heard what he said and looked towards him; they were laughing. I had never said a word to Vimanshu before as I never gave him that much importance.

"Whatever you want to say, say it upfront! Do not whisper like a girl!" I said.

"At least I don't go behind girls like you do," he said.

This statement hurt me deeply. I got up and went towards his bench.

"Who are you? Who the fuck are you? Asshole!" I said in anger standing there, looking right into his eyes.

"Ask her what I am!" he said.

I held his collar and told him to walk outside the class. He remained on his seat knowing what could happen with him now. He was acting like a pussy at that moment. Sir looked behind at us and he understood what was going on in there. He immediately ordered me to take my seat.

Now it was a waiting game for me as I really wanted to kick his ass through the curve. The bell rang to end the last period of the day.

It was the rule of our school that first the ground floor students will get out of the class, then the first floor, and then the second floor. All the students had to follow one queue and move forward to the parking area. It was applied to stop the rush of the students in the school premises.

So we had a five-minute window to fight. First the girls of the class moved out of the class. Everybody had seen me holding his collar. So they all knew what was going to happen.

Shikha was looking at me and I didn't want to look at her. I was totally disgusted with her by now, and the moment I looked at her, I could see her face with anticipation of what follows next. It was a mistake to look at her as it increased my anger more. As soon as all the girls went out of the class, I went to his bench. He was standing there. The other boys were standing three feet away from us. I went close to him.

"Bastard! What you were saying?" I said calmly.

"I told whatever I wanted to," Vimanshu said in arrogance.

"Do you know whom you are talking to?" I said and reminded him of my status in school.

"Yes," he said with a straight face.

"I will tear you from the middle," I said and moved closer to him and put my finger on his chest.

"Do you have the guts to do that? You can't even handle a girl. Look how she rejected you," he said.

The moment he said that, I punched him on his face with full force. He tried to punch me too, but I held his hand. At the same moment, I felt a punch on my back. I turned back and saw Shubham holding Kuldeep's collar shoving him away.

I felt another punch on my chest by Vimanshu and I punched him on his shoulder joint. He shrieked in pain.

It happened very fast and it made so much noise that it attracted the attention of a teacher standing outside our class room. He came into our class.

"What is happening?" the teacher shouted.

We saw him and quickly moved to take our bags and joined the students' queue as we were aware of the rule of the school. The rule was that if a student from tenth class breaks any disciplinary law, he was to be suspended and was not allowed to sit for the board exams.

"You saw them. They were just standing," Shubham said in the queue.

"Yeah man! Sameer and Vinay, right?" I asked.

"Yeah," he said.

Sameer and Vinay stood there watching the full incident. I was not expecting them to cover for me, but I saw them standing there and not doing anything.

It hurt me as they were my long time friends and as a friend you are expected to at least support your friend. This was the last time I expected anything from them as our friendship was over after this incident. Till this date, I have never approached them by myself.

Two years later in 2010, I was in Kota preparing for the IIT entrance exam in Bansal Institute. One day I was walking with my friend Riddhima along the Indra Vihar Road in Kota. I saw Vimanshu standing at a juice corner. I looked at him and ignored him and moved forward.

"Sudhanshu!" he shouted from behind.

I looked at him. He was standing alone. He came running to me.

"How are you?" he said and seemed excited to see me.

"I am good," I said.

"He is from my school," I told Riddhima, a friend of mine and girlfriend of my friend Shubham Sinha.

They exchanged hellos. I was standing silently as I was really in no mood to talk with him. Meanwhile, he said something which showed his class.

He patted me on my shoulder and asked if she was my girlfriend. It really looked cheap. Riddhima looked at me and laughed.

"What do you think?" she asked Vimanshu.

She was really a cocky girl. I will just say that she was absolutely a copy of Bani from the show *Roadies*. She was from Delhi and had tattoos twice the number of her age on her body.

He remained silent. He looked at her, then at me, and then at her. He was in complete shock, to see a girl with such confidence and personality. He ignored her and didn't reply.

I stood there for a few seconds and took Riddhima's hand in mine hand and continued walking. Riddhima knew my story and when I reminded her that he was 'that Vimanshu', she was surprised and asked me, "How the hell can anybody be attracted to him?"

I laughed at her question and said, "Yeah, tell me about it."

Sameer's Misery

AS DESCRIBED EARLIER IN THE BOOK, SAMEER AND his brother used to live in a rented room in Dumra. Their parents used to live in the village in Sitamarhi. It was tough for them to live in one room where they used to cook, sleep, study and keep their belongings.

We were great friends, so I used to go at his place and used to spend a lot of time as there was no guardian to monitor us. It remained my favourite spot for relaxing for the longest time.

I, along with our other friends, used to gather there. We'd cook and celebrate every small and big occasion together.

Sometimes Sameer's mom used to come to stay with them. Whenever she'd come, she used to call me for lunch. I was very close to his mother and his sister. They used to love me like Sameer and I used to love them like my own family.

We were not on the talking terms with each other after the incident with Vimanshu.

It was the rainy season and it was raining heavily that day. Sitamarhi is situated on the banks of the river Bagmati and floods were a common problem every year.

Floods were devastating this time. Many villages were cut off from each other.

Sameer's village was also one of them.

One day Sameer came to my house. It was raining heavily on that day with strong winds which could blow anything away with its power.

"Ramu, where is Anand?" he asked all soaked.

Ramu was the guy who used to work in my home. He was more like a friend to me than a servant. He knew that I was avoiding him because I told him about everything which had taken place till.

"Bhaiya is not here, he went out," Ramu lied.

"In this weather?" he asked.

"Yeah!" Ramu said and nodded convincingly.

"Ramu, it's urgent. I know he is inside the house. Tell him my mother is calling him," he said.

I could hear him from my room. I went outside to the main gate.

"What happened?" I said in anger.

"What Anand? You will not even talk to me?" he asked.

"You deserve it man!" I said.

He stood there silently.

"What happened? Why is Aunty calling me?" I shouted.

"There's a problem," he said.

I didn't want to know about his problem. I had nothing to do with this person, but since he took his mother's name, so I asked.

"What problem?" I asked.

"You wouldn't believe me," he said. "We need money," he added.

"Really, dude?" I said. This guy had no shame.

"I knew you will not believe me. We are cut off from my family because of the floods. If you have no faith in me, then you can come with me and ask my mother," he said.

This was not the first time he had asked me for money. I had helped him few times before. I could have given him the money up front, but this time we were on the completely different paths and I had no faith in him any longer.

So I decided to go to his home despite the weather. I reached his room and saw Aunty there. I touched her feet.

"Stay blessed," she said. "How are you beta?"

"I am fine Aunty. How you are?" I said.

"I am good beta."

"When did you come?" I asked.

"It's been over a month now. I have been stuck here due to the floods. Your uncle is alone there," she said with concern on her face.

"Ohk… he was telling me about money, Aunty," I said gesturing towards Sameer.

"Yes beta. If you can help, it would be really nice, as we don't know anyone here except you. I will return you the money later," she said.

I took out a five hundred rupee note and gave it to her. It was from my own savings.

"Thank you beta!"

"Aunty, if you need more, inform me without any hesitation," I said.

"I think this will be enough beta."

"Okay Aunty, I am leaving," I said.

"No beta, where are you going in this weather? Wait, I will make something for you," she said.

"It's okay," I said.

"Beta, he told me that you both are not talking with each other."

"It's not like that Aunty. He is a grown man now… he knows what he needs," I said.

"Do not fight beta. Sort out your differences and be friends like before," she said.

"I don't think that will happen," I said.

"But beta…" she said.

"Okay, Aunty I am leaving," I said.

I touched her feet and went out of the building. This was the last time I spoke to Aunty. Also, this was the last time I met Sameer. Although we used to be in the same class, I avoided him throughout the tenth class, till the present day.

Letter to Mansi

THREE MONTHS HAD PASSED AFTER MY KOLKATA trip. I was halfway through to regain myself. The only possible way to completely recover was to move on in life. And the only possible way to forget the past and move on in life was to get in contact with Mansi again.

It was not like I was not trying. Actually I had asked Aakriti about Mansi and had asked whether she would be coming to the coaching classes again or not. She always replied positively, but Mansi never came.

So at last I decided to write a letter to her so that at least after reading it she would come to class again.

Dear Mansi,

Hi.
Well this must be unexpected for you. There are no poetic words to say I miss you. So I will simply say that I miss you.

It's funny how things change around you. And it's true that you get to know the value of someone when they are not around you.

You know I still remember your words "I like you but not more than your happiness". Now I will say that my happiness is lost and I think you are the only person where I can find it. And also, you can help me redefine myself.

I need you. And I like you.
I hope you still like me.

Your crush,
Sudhanshu Anand

I put the letter in an envelope and put it in the notebook. I went to the coaching centre to give it to Aakriti. I entered the class and saw Aakriti sitting with Kurtika. I gave the notebook to her and told her to give it to Mansi.

I had not attended class that day and came just to give the letter to her. Rishikesh sir looked at me with suspicion.

"Why didn't you come for the classes today?" he asked.

"Sir I have some work at my home. I just came to give her the notebook," I said.

He didn't say anything after that, but I knew he had understood everything. I went out of the class and pretty much felt like a typical movie hero after doing this.

❖

Now it was time for me to wait for her reply. I knew I had not behaved well with her for almost a month after the fight with Aakriti. But somehow I had the satisfaction that since Aakriti was now in touch with me, then she shouldn't have a problem.

But still, I was nervous and restless for her reply. Next day, I reached a little late, so class had already started. Rumit sir was teaching physics.

I looked at Aakriti. I looked at her and gestured that we'd talk after the class. Now it was again a waiting game for me.

Luckily the class ended before time. She gave me the notebook while sitting on her seat. She smiled, so that was a good sign for me.

I saw a letter inside the notebook. I became happy as she had replied. My excitement was absolutely on another level at that moment. I had felt the same excitement when I first saw her on 'that' rainy day.

I was sitting on the bench with the other guys, so it was difficult for me to read the letter there. So I decided that I would read it at home. It was the last class of the day.

We were waiting for Rajesh sir to come. Five minutes passed, ten minutes passed, fifteen minutes passed, but there was no sign of him. It was not going well with me. With each passing minute, my anxiety to read the letter was getting higher.

I went out of the class to look for Rajesh sir, but he was not in the office at that time. So I went to another class where Rishikesh sir was teaching. I asked him about Rajesh sir, and he said that he was absent.

I was happy to hear him and rushed to my class and informed all the students.

Aakriti went out of the class in a hurry. I noticed that, but didn't say anything as I was excited about the letter.

So I rushed home on my bicycle. I went directly to my room. I took the letter out of the notebook and started to read it.

Dear Sudhanshu,

I gave your letter to Mansi but she tore it into two pieces and didn't even read it. I know you are a good guy.

Whatever you think about Mansi, she is not like that. She is completely different and doesn't care about your feelings.

She used to talk with you only because she wanted your help in her studies. Also, she wanted to be with you because you are famous in school.

I again rearranged your letter and read it in front of her. Throughout the letter, she was laughing and was saying that I don't care about him.

She also told me, "Has he seen his face in the mirror? Why will I like him?"

I am only writing this letter because I care about you. She even asked me to not write this letter as you don't matter to her.

Listen, you are a good guy, so I will advise you to not waste your time on a girl like her.

I hope you understand what I am trying to say.

Your friend,
Aakriti Singh

I was sweating. I had an intuition that this was not Mansi's behaviour. But it was the end of my expectations from Mansi, at least for that moment, as it put doubts in my mind about her. I was stunned and at the same time angry about what kind of person writes this kind of letter to anybody.

Honestly, I thought that it had been over nine months, while people can change within a few days. I had also seen Shikha changing completely, which made me have doubts about Mansi too.

Phone calls to Mansi

MANSI WAS STILL NOT COMING TO THE COACHING classes, despite the letter I gave her through Aakriti.

I knew Mansi would never do such a thing described by Aakriti in her letter. At least she would have written a letter herself in response.

I was in great confusion at that time. If Mansi didn't want to even write a letter to me, then why did Aakriti take the responsibility of writing it.

She was the first reason due to which I lost contact with Mansi, and last I remember, Mansi always tried to start talking with me. So it put me in the strange situation of whom to believe and whom to not.

So I went to Shubham's house to meet him and sort out this confusion. I handed him the letter to read. He read it in front of me.

"I can't believe it," he said with disbelief in his eyes.

"Yeah, tell me about it," I said.

"What do you think?" he asked.

"I don't know man. Whom should I believe and what I should believe?" I said rubbing my eyes.

"I think Aakriti didn't give your letter to Mansi," he said after a few seconds.

"You think so?" I said as I also wanted him to feel that way, to release some pressure off me.

"Man! I have seen Mansi. She is a very different girl. Whatever Aakriti has written about her in this letter, that is not how she'd react," he said with full confidence.

"I know."

"And also, Aakriti doesn't want you to be with her in the first place," he said. "She is not a trustworthy girl," he added.

"Another important thing is why she will take the responsibility of even replying if Mansi didn't want to?" he asked.

"Okay, but why is Mansi not coming? At least she can come for one day, just to talk with me," I said to cross check his words.

"Don't worry. I am sure she will find a way to contact you," he said assuringly.

And she did find a way to communicate with me. A few days later, as I was getting out of the classroom, I saw Kurtika standing at the stairs and looking at me.

"Hi Anand" she said waving.

"Hi, what happened?" I asked rudely.

"Actually, Mansi had asked for your number," she said.

"Why? She can't even reply to my letter, but she wants my number," I said in irritation.

"No, it's not like that," she said.

"What do you mean?" I said.

"You also think like this? You know her better," she said.

There was silence for a moment.

"Aakriti never gave the letter to her and whatever she had written…," she continued.

"How do you know this?" I asked in anticipation.

"Because I was with her when Aakriti wrote the letter and she also told me not to tell Mansi about it. But Mansi is my friend and close to me, so I told her. Mansi wants your number so that she can talk to you."

"But I still have not understood why Aakriti would not give the letter to Mansi?" I asked.

"Because they are having disputes in their family and both of them have not been talking for months now," she said.

"Ohkay!" I said in sheer relief.

I wrote my landline number on her hand.

"Thank you," she said.

"Arrey… don't mention. Actually I should thank you for the help," I said.

She smiled.

It was Sunday afternoon. A landline number appeared on the caller ID set up of my telephone. I picked the call as I was expecting Mansi's call.

"Hello," I said.

"Hello, Anand?" Kurtika said.

"Yes, and you are? I said to confirm who it was.

"Kurtika!" she said.

"Oh yes, hi," I said.

"What are you doing right now?" she asked.

"Nothing, I was just in my room, playing with my dog."

"Oh wow, what kind of dog do you have?" she asked.

"He is a white fur Pomeranian." I said.

"Wow, he must be cute then," she said.

"Yes, he is very cute, but he is dangerous also. He will first attract you with his cuteness, then after you end pampering him, he will bite you," I said.

"Oh my god, really?" she said.

"Hmm!" I said and smiled.

"Okay, someone wants to talk," she said in excitement.

"Hi," Mansi said in a second.

"Hi, how are you?" I said.

"I am fine. How are you?"

"Not good," I said.

"Why? What happened?" she asked.

"Yaar, I sent you a letter. Did you get it?" I asked.

"No," she said and laughed.

"Akriti hasn't been talking to me since two months as there have been some family problems," she continued.

"Why? What happened?" I asked.

"Nothing, it's usual in our family. Leave it, otherwise you will get bored."

"Okay, it's been a long time since I heard your voice," I said.

"Yes, I was going to say exactly that."

"Why have you not been coming?" I asked.

"It's a long story," she said.

"Hmm… I have enough time to listen," I said.

"Well, my father lives in Patna, which leaves me, my mom and my brother here. She gets anxious sometimes and lately she has been ill most of the time. So I remain at my home to look after her," she said.

"Oh, how is she now?" I asked.

"She is fine now," she said.

"If you need any help, I mean if you need me, I am here," I said.

"I know."

"I miss you," I said.

"Liar," she said.

"Arrey… why'll I lie to you?" I said.

"Why do you miss me?"

"It's a very good question, but these things are not discussed on the telephone, madam," I said.

"Okay, tell me why you stopped talking to me."

"You know the reason," I said.

"But you had the fight with her."

"Yeah, I know, but you know how I am."

"Whatever I said about eyes and peanuts on that day was for you. Why did she get agitated?" I added.

"That was for me?" she asked in surprise.

"Yes, it was for you," I said.

"You compared my eyes with peanuts?" she said.

"Yes, I think your eyes are like peanuts. Well I like your eyes," I said with a laugh.

"Ah… you think that?" she said.

"Hmm. So how are your studies going?" I added.

"I am managing," she said.

"I have not seen you in school lately. Why?" I asked.

"Yes, same reason, but I am trying my best to attend school," she said.

"If you need any help, let me know," I offered.

"Thanks."

"Listen, tell Kurtika to take the letter from Aakriti," I said.

"I don't think she will give the letter to her," she said.

"Don't tell her that you are asking for it. Tell Kurtika to take the letter when she is not around," I said.

"Okay, I will see you tomorrow, in school," she said.

I disconnected the call with a big smile.

Mansi in my Section

I WAS GETTING BETTER AS MANSI WAS IN CONTACT with me constantly. Shubham was also there for me. Everything was going in the right direction now.

Being in touch with Mansi gradually brought back the old me. Although the Shikha chapter was over in my mind, but it was quite evident that its impact would remain on my life.

It was raining since day broke. Due to the rain, very few student came to school. Whenever there were few students, two sections used to be merged. That day, section D was going to be combined with our section C.

It was great for me as Mansi was in section D and we had the opportunity to spend an entire day in the same class.

Mansi went directly to my bench. It was quite evident that Mansi took my seat purposely. Shikha was keeping an eye on every move Mansi was making.

Most of the students of the section D knew me and some of them were my good friends. I was in section D for one year in fifth class before I was transferred to the section C.

I was sitting with Shubham and with my section D friends in the last benches and I could see Mansi sitting in front of me in the row to my left.

She was trying her best to look at me. Actually she was making a fake conversation with the girl beside her and was looking continuously at me. Shikha was noticing it.

I looked at Shikha and I could see her face. The look on her face brought memories. Actually I could see Shikha in the same frame of mind that I had been when Shikha was taking interest in Vimanshu.

I looked at Mansi and she looked right into my eyes.

I also started to look into her eyes. I was also shaking my head from time to time so that sir didn't get what actually was going on there. Mansi leaned her head on the bag and started to stare at me.

Her friend tapped her on her shoulder to end her lustful stare. She ignored her and again started to stare. I took my eyes off her and looked at Shikha. She was looking at me questioningly.

I saw her glance and looked away in anger. She was reaping what she had sowed. She was haplessly sitting there. She remained in the same phase throughout the day and didn't look at Vimanshu that day.

"Hello," I said.

"Hi, what are you doing?" Mansi asked over a call that evening.

"Nothing important! I was just thinking about you," I said.

"Oh, same here! Do you know, when they asked us to go to your section, I almost jumped out of my bench," she said.

"I was surprised to see you coming in our classes," I said.

"I wanted to sit on your bench so I purposely went to your seat," she said.

"Yeah, I noticed it," I said.

"You should have seen Shikha's face! Oh my god, it had become red with jealousy," she said with quite a feminine laugh.

"Oh that," I said with a smile.

"I thought you'd sit behind me," she said.

"Actually I also wanted to sit there, but my friends called me to sit with them," I said.

"Hmm… every teacher knows who you are?" she asked.

"They know me through my brother. My brother is a scholar student and they think I am his rogue brother," I said.

"Well, definitely you are a naughty one, but quite likeable though," she said.

"But I have still not done anything naughty with you," I said.

"Haw… you are bad."

"Hmm!" I said.

"Hmm!"

"Let's meet somewhere," I said.

"Why?"

"Just to show you how naughty I am," I said.

She didn't say anything.

"Just to spend time together," I said.

"But, where?" she asked.

"At home!" I suggested.

"What about your family?"

"There is no problem, you can come," I said.

"No, it will not look good."

"Don't worry, my family doesn't think too much. They are easy going people," I said.

"No, believe me, I will be not comfortable," she said.

"Okay, then you decide the place."

"We will meet after the exam as I—"

The call got disconnected. She usually did that when her mother was around.

Love Never Dies

IT WAS THE END OF OUR TENTH BOARD EXAMS. I had already planned with Mansi way before the start of the exams to meet her in person after the exams. So I called her.

"Hello," she said.

"How was your exam?" I asked.

"It went well. Yours?"

"Better than the other exams," I said.

"Good."

"Now when we are meeting?" I asked.

"Okay, when are you going to Kota?" she asked.

"I have my entrance exam on 2nd April in Kolkata, so I will take the train on the night of 1st April. Then I will return on the afternoon of 3rd April," I said.

"No, I mean, when will you be leaving for Kota?"

"On 9th April," I said.

"Then we could meet on the fourth," she said.

"Nice, but I have only two days to plan," I said.

"Plan what?" she asked.

"That is a surprise," I said.

"Don't over think and overdo, and by the way, what are you planning?" she sked suspiciously.

I knew immediately why she had reacted in this way. Honestly, I was not thinking much about it, but her suspicion gave me the idea.

"Well, I have to look for a place where we can have lunch. Also, I have to look for a place where we both can spend some quality time before I leave this place," I said.

"Okay. But don't plan too much in case I'm unable to come."

"Don't say that. You have to come, otherwise I will come to your house and will take you with me in front of your mother and brother."

"That will not be necessary," she said with a cute laugh.

"Listen, you have to come at eleven towards no 3, where it ends and meets with Shankar Chowk. I will be waiting opposite the temple. I will be on a red-coloured bike and if you see me, then you have to make a gesture with your hand," I said.

"Okay, I will be wearing a white suit with a red dupatta and I will be covering my face with a scarf. When I see you, I will wave my hand," she said.

"Okay madam. I have bought a present for you. I hope you will like it," I said.

It was a slip of tongue as it was supposed to be a surprise for her.

"Don't worry, I will love it," she said.

"Okay listen, I have to go. I have to make a lot of arrangements," I said.

"Wait, I love you. Do you love me?" she asked.

"I will answer this question when we meet," I said before saying goodbye.

There were plenty of things on my plate for the next few days. I went out to look for a place where we could have lunch. Soon I found one and booked a table for us for 4th April. It was the best restaurant in Sitamarhi. To spend some quality time together, I thought of my house. I didn't want to tell her about it, otherwise she would have said no.

On the 1st morning, I took a bus to reach Patna with my friends who were also coming along with me to appear for the entrance exam of Bansal classes. We booked tickets on the same Rajdhani Express to reach Kolkata.

We reached Kolkata at six in the morning. My brother was there at the station to pick me up. I went with him to his college Maritime University and the other guys went out to the hotel arranged by him.

I had breakfast in his room and rested there. Bhaiya returned from class at eleven in the morning. I had freshened up and was watching movies on his laptop.

My exam was at four, so we left the college at two. The exam was in some old school. We reached at half past three. My friends were already there.

The exam went well. Our train was at half past seven in the evening, so we all went to the railway station as soon as possible. My brother saw us off and we took our seats in the train. I was excited a day later, I would be meeting Mansi in person.

On the morning of 4th April, I woke up at seven. I got fresh as soon as possible and went to the petrol pump to fill the petrol tank of the bike. On the way, I bought a bouquet for her. I put my best clothes on and sprayed a nice perfume.

At 10:50, I left my home as the temple at Shankar Chowk was just a minute away. I reached and began to wait for her. I was really excited and was constantly looking at the end of road number three. I was looking at my watch every few seconds; it felt like time had stopped.

I saw one girl emerging from behind the wall of one building which had covered the view of the road. She was wearing a white suit with a red dupatta and had a white scarf on her face. She was tall, thin and had long hair.

I immediately understood that it was her. She looked towards me and then towards the other side. She again looked towards my side, but was unable to see me. I realised I was wearing a helmet.

I unlocked the button of my helmet and closed my eyes to take it off. That moment, I heard an explosion. I took my helmet off and looked in the direction in which Mansi was standing.

I saw a cloud of dust settling down slowly. A Bolero car had hit the wall. The guy in the car was badly injured. Mansi had been standing right there. I couldn't see her, so I left my bike at the temple and ran towards the road.

People had gathered all around the car by then. I saw Mansi lying on the corner of road number three. She was not moving. I saw her eyes closing. She took a huge mouthful of air before life ebbed out of her body.

Facebook Chat
with Shikha (2014)

I HAD JUST SHIFTED FROM THE PDPU (UG) HOSTEL to my brand new three BHK flat in Gokul Baugh Apartment in Kudasen, Gandhinagar. In the beginning, I, with my friend Rakesh Roshan, were among the four guys who had shifted, and we had the responsibility to make all the arrangements to make the flat a home for four of us college boys.

Yeah, you hear the name right, Rakesh Roshan. He was the guy with quite a 'sexy' figure. He was rather thin and wore spectacles. He was a good friend of mine.

We had successfully installed the 'Tikona Internet service' in our flat that day to fulfil our daily dose of social entertainment. We had had a very long day, so we all were quite tired. My other friend Deepanshu, a typical Jaipur guy, had come to help us along with Negi, a junior guy from Himachal Pradesh, with the behaviour of a wannabe Delhi guy.

Another great support was my Gujarati 'mama'. His name was Vinu Hada, a typical Gujarati man who had a tea stall just beside our apartment. We used to go to his stall in the mornings and evenings to drink tea and chat.

He had a ten-year-old boy Prateek and a six-year-old daughter Jinal. In the night, we had dinner brought by both the beautiful kids, made by mama's wife.

After they left our house, it was time to use the newly installed internet in our flat. We had decided that we will use it alternate days and one by one because we wanted good speed. It was Rakesh's turn to use it first, but I asked him to let me, as I wanted to check some emails.

The moment I connected my laptop with the internet, I saw many notifications from Facebook. So the first thing I did was to click on the 'messages' bar of Facebook. I saw one message from Shikha. The following is the conversation between us over four days.

Hi. Shikha messaged.

Me: *hi how are you?*

S: *good. What about you?*

Me: *All good here, so how is college going?*

S: *Nice. How is life?*

Me: *Life is ok, how is your brother and uncle, aunty?*

S: *Superb. How is your family?*

Me: *They are good.*

S: *So what's up?*

Me: *Nothing much*

S: *Ohkk*

Me: *By the way, you look good in your pics.*

S: *Lolz, thank you.*

Me: *That was a compliment.*

S: *I said thank you. You have changed.*

Me: *Yeah right.*

S: *Went through your profile. So, said that.*

Me: *Okkk. But you only got to see my pics. Anyway tell me about your life?*

S: *All good. What about you?*

Me: *Fine. It's been a long time since we talked.*

S: *Ya… too long. Are you there? Or left?*

Me: *Sorry. I went through your profile right now which brought back some memories.*

S: *Memories about??*

Me: *You and me, what else.*

S: *Oh, so what about you present?*

Me: *What about my present? Come on, you can ask me anything freely…*

S: *Gf? Bf?*

Me: *Bf, he is the love of my life. We are getting married.*

S: *Hehehehe, don't forget to invite me.*

Me: *Only men allowed.*

S: *You mean…? I will change my get up.*

Me: *No seriously, what do you wanna hear, ye or ne about a Gf?*

S: *The truth.*

Me: *I always speak the truth.*

S: *So reply…*

Me: *Right now I am not dating anybody, what about you?*

S: *Means you are dating someone.*

Me: *It's been sometime. What about you?*

S: *Sometime… what time?*

Me: *You are not answering my question, what about you?*

S: *What if I don't answer? How is college going? Your sis?*

Me: *Then I will take it as a yes.*

S: *Your wish.*

Me: *Wish…? Sis is good. She is in college right now.*

S: *Great!! I mean it's your choice, you can think whatever you want…*

Me: *Now you are talking like Salman.*

S: *You may say that… I am a Salman fan.*

Me: *I don't like that person. (Although I am a big fan of him.)*

S: *Hey…after 12, I won't be able to chat… wifi sucks… so don't think I am ignoring you.*

Me: *Don't worry, I will not. But change your wifi then…*

S: *That's not possible.*

Me: *Don't tell me it's Salman's wifi.*

S: *Pj…*

Me: *So do you believe what I had told you two years ago?*

S: *I don't know… actually I don't want to know… it's all okay now… I don't have any grudge against you…*

Me: *I just wanted to make you feel the way you do now at that time. Anyway, I missed your dimples.*

S: *Thanks for the concern… you missed them?*

Me: *Ya, are they okay? Jesus, your wifi does suck…*

S: *You there?*

S: *?*

Me: *You online?*

S: *Yo yo*

Me: *Cool. What's wrong with your wifi?*

S: *Nothing*

Me: *You became offline around twelve…*

S: *Ya that's my time to get offline.*

S: *How was your day?*

Me: *Had classes till 6 p.m.*

S: *Lolz enjoy.*

Me: *Yeah right… your classes?*

S: *Bunked*

Me: *Don't tell me you bunked your classes to sleep.*

S: *Nah… I was not feeling well.*

Me: *What happened? Are you ok?*

S: *Nothing much. Leave it.*

Me: *Okkk left it.*

S: *Thank you.*

Me: *Your wifi is gonna work today?*

S: *Ya I guess.*

Me: *Excellent. So how is Bhubaneswar as a city?*

S: *Very bad.*

Me: *Why?*

S: *Too hot, too boring.*

Me: *Boring in the sense?*

S: *There aren't any good places to hang out.*

Me: *what about Udaygiri and Khandgiri caves?*

S: *nice… but not awesome…*

Me: *okkk define awesome…*

S: *somethings can't be expressed.*

Me: *so there is nothing in Bubhneshwar which can't be expressed?*

S: *no.*

Me: *I know one place there which is awesome.*

S: *And that is…*

Me: *When I will go there, I will show you.*

S: *Happy friendship day.*

Me: *Today is friendship's day? I hate your wifi.*

S: *You don't need to hate it… I am back…*

Me: *You watch sitcoms?*

S: *I am too busy… no time for such stuff.*

Me: *Busy to bunk classes…*

S: *Nah, to hang out with friends…*

Me: *From where, a fan or a well?*

S: *Your pjs suck.*

Me: *Oh come on, that was good.*

S: *No…*

S: *There?*

Me: *Yup*

S: *Sorry… I am a little busy.*

Me: *Doing what?*

S: *With friends.*

Me: *Okkk*

S: *What are you doing?*

Me: *Watching videos on YouTube.*

S: *What videos?*

Me: *About children in Syria.*

S: *Oh… send me the link.*

S: *Will watch later.*

Me: *Fine.*

S: *Can I ask you something if you don't mind?*

Me: *Yup.*

S: *Don't you dare lie.*

Me: *I will not.*

S: *What was there between you and Mansi?*

Me: *I told you there was nothing. It was hyped by the other girls in the coaching classes.*

S: *Don't lie…*

Me: *Why should I lie? Believe me for one time. Do you wanna know what really happened?*

S: *Ohkk… nah not interested…*

Me: *Good.*

S: *So… tell me something new.*

Me: *You chat with Shubham, what do you wanna know?*

S: *Anything.*

Me: *Went to Diu with friends and had fun, classes started now, so not having fun.*

S: *Great!*

Me: *It was great then now it's not so great.*

S: *You there?*

That's it. It was the last time we chatted or had any kind of communication. I think I don't have to give any reason to why I stopped messaging her.

The conversation itself describes my resistance to not text her anymore.

Letter to Mansi

Dear Mansi,

It seems like yesterday I called you for the last time and for the last time we spoke to each other. There was so much to tell you and there still is, but it was always 'time and place' between us.

It was complicated back then, but one thing was sure that I was in love with Shikha, and at the same time, I wanted to be friends with you. Later it changed and we became extremely close for some time.

The truth is, I wanted to be close to you since the first time I saw you, but I knew that it would not be appropriate. So I never tried to. I had described the moment when I first saw you; I hope I have done justice.

Whatever short time we got to spend together is very dear to me. You were a beautiful part of my life and whenever I think about you, a beautiful face with a cute smile comes across my eyes.

It must not have been easy for you to tolerate all the bullshit said around you. The way you handled it was quite exceptional. You never were frightened and never even got irritated by it.

More importantly, I wish I could have had more time with you; but it's harsh reality that it was not meant to happen.

Sometimes people need to be selfish. I never used to believe this statement, but now I do. Because if I would have been a little more selfish, or you would have been a little more selfish, then we could have created a different ending to this story.

I am doing well now and I hope you will be satisfied with whatever I have achieved in my life until now. If given a chance, I would like to give up everything just to have a minute more with you…so that I could tell you 'I love you too'.

You were a strong girl and would have been a strong woman by now. I hope to see you on the other side.

Letter to Amrita

Hi, how are you?

This is incredible. I am writing this letter on the Christmas eve and we had celebrated this day in 2007, nine years ago, by going to church in Sitamarhi.

I wonder how you look now. The reason I said this is because I remember you as a girl with short hair in jeans and a t-shirt, a tomboy.

When I met you for the first time in our coaching classes, you seemed to be an interesting girl with a strong opinion about all the subjects we used to discuss, but it had changed drastically the last time I heard you.

It's remarkable that a strong opinionated girl like you never said anything directly to me, but said all that bullshit about me and my loved ones in front of other people. Sometimes, people should think before speaking and you should also have done that.

It's hurtful and at the same time I was disgusted with myself that I ever called you a friend. You never expect a friend to make another friend's life a living hell.

You knew Shubham Aashu liked you and I'd never do anything against him or hurt him. More importantly, I was with Shikha, but still you tried every disgusting tactic with a shitty girl like Kamini Priya.

The only reason I wanted to write this letter to you is because of the first impression I had of you.

Everyone in this world gets rejected, but they don't go nuts and try to destroy everything beautiful around them. It's just the way life is sometimes and we should try to make peace with it.

Letter to Siddharth

Hi brother, how are you?

I know when you will read this letter, you will be having a great smile on your face, and believe me, I am writing this letter with the same smile on my face.

I miss you buddy, and I missed you a lot when you left our school. Although we had chatted on WhatsApp and had called each other recently, but jeez, that time was different.

I still cherish and remember all the memories we had together, along with Sameer.

The moments where we used to wait for the lunch break and used to go after the girls of section A. Our hairstyles were so important for us. We used to talk for hours, just about how to maintain a hairstyle.

Remember we'd come to school with a comb and Fair & Lovely cream to get ready before lunch. So we could look fresh and better in front of the girls. We used to irritate the teachers so that they'd throw us out of the class and we could save ourselves from their boring lectures.

Constantly getting out of the class and bunking the whole period, roaming around the school, sitting for hours in the school field were our priorities; studying was definitely not.

Roaming on our bikes around Dumra, eating snacks at our regular places, talking hours about the girls passing by were other things we loved.

Another important aspect for us was music. It was another thread in our bonding. How we loved singing and jamming together.

I wish we could have started our own band. By the way, I still have the notebook on which we used to write songs of our favourite musicians and the one song we wrote together and promised each other to work together on.

I never said this in front of you, but I loved your singing, man, and also the way you used to perform.

You have had a great impact on this novel also, even by not being involved in it. In fact, when you left our school it broke our pack and later affected my friendship with Sameer, which had a great impact all throughout the story.

Letter to Sameer

Hi, how are you?

I remember the first time we met in the fifth class. You were standing along the route of our school and you asked me for a lift on my bicycle.

It's amazing. If I would have not applied the brakes on my bicycle, we would not have been friends of that calibre or shared the same bonding, I think you will also agree to this.

The second day, I saw you again at the same place, then I understood immediately that again you would ask me for a lift. You did. You saw me and waved at me. And since that meeting, we have been friends for a very long time.

Although we didn't belong to the same section, you told me that you knew me as the topper of section D. You told me about your family and the difficulties you were facing to attend school by living away from your parents.

The same day, you came home after school to play cricket in our division 'I' colony. It was an instant bonding between us and soon we started to enjoy each other's company.

The middle part of our friendship was excellent. We have enough memories together to cherish throughout our lives. Meeting your sis and mom was amazing. They felt like my own family and I expected the same from you when you used to come home.

It's not important who helped more and how much. And I think we should not count it; otherwise it would be cheap manipulation of our friendship.

The only problem I have with you now, which I would never be able to digest, is that I called you brother and treated you as a brother. I treated your family as my own, but how on earth could you get influenced by those fucking idiots against your brother! You put our friendship aside.

Listen man, I am nobody to forgive you for what you did and I don't want your apologies. It's just that I am happy at my place and you are happy at yours.

Letter to Shubham Aashu

Hi brother, how are you?

This is not easy for me to write. You know it's tough to write about a person whom you consider a part of your family. It's tough because you don't know where to start.

Well, I know you, brother, since I was in class fourth, when you were studying with my elder brother in the fifth. Initially I thought you were an annoying fat guy with no humour and this remained my perception of you for a very long time.

True friendship or true brotherhood can be understood when the person stands by you in all situations, whether good or bad. I think everyone will agree with this statement.

Believe me, I never expected any kind of support from you as I was never good to you. I used to fight with you, even when it wasn't your fault. But you remained with me through all those bad times and you gave me the support which I needed at that time.

You remained with me even when all the odds were against me and when all my other friends left me. You did this even when people used to say there was something going on between me and Amrita. This is quite appreciable. You are a strong person with a clear head.

I learned a lot from you, brother, and you know I can do anything for you if it's in my capacity. The reason I called you brother is because I have a great amount of respect for you and you know it.

Letter to Shikha

Dear Shikha,

I don't know where to start. Alright, the art of writing developed in me, thanks to you. Yes, you are the reason and I wish I could tell you that this is the hardest thing I have written so far.

But you changed me as a person. Before I met you, I was a usual teenager who was going crazy offbeat. I was doing all the childish activities any teenager indulged in.

Since I met you, there have been a lot of changes, and this is the statement made by my mother.

We were in the same class since April 2004, but we never even looked at each other. It's funny how things around you change. There was a chance of losing you, but anyhow, I got you in my life.

Change is the law of life. What you think, what you are and what you are gonna be, these are three different important aspects of life.

There are challenges in a relationship. Now when I look back and understand the whole situation, the only reason for our separation comes to me that we didn't push our limits and ourselves to the extremities. Another factor for us was maturity.

Yes, we were mature enough to love each other, but not enough to save our relationship; otherwise these fucking idiots would have been invisible.

After our separation, there were many sleepless nights for me, but one thing was for sure, you remained in each dream in whatever little sleep I got.

I always told you the truth. You never asked me directly about Mansi at any point. Since there was lack of communication between us, you got influenced by those idiots.

During the time we were together, Mansi and I never crossed that line although we could have easily done so.

Yes, I used to like her and also wanted to get close and be more than a friend with her, but not when we were in a relationship. I kept her aside during our 'us' time.

We became close when you were not talking to me and found interest in another guy. Yes, I observed that and you know the guy's name.

Mansi was a nice girl; a good friend, who never got influenced by anyone. I can give you an example: I saw you talking to her in school one day in the morning. I asked her what you were asking. She didn't tell me anything and said that she'd never tell me.

The most important thing is that I never informed you about Mansi's demise as somewhere you didn't deserve to know about her.

You can always blame me for what happened and you can say whatever you want to, but I tried more than enough times to reconcile with you. But you went into a very different zone and got influenced by the stupid people around you.

On the last day of our tenth board exams, I wanted to talk with you, but something within me stopped me. I think I don't like saying goodbye. So I never said goodbye to you.

I called you when I was in Kota just because I wanted you to know the truth and be proud of our relationship and time together.

When you texted me on Facebook in 2014, I was pleasantly surprised. I was happy that finally you had overcome all those bad memories. I wanted to chat and talk more, but I was involved in a relationship at that time. So I backed out and stopped.

I know you would say that we could have been friends since then, but I don't want you to be just a friend. I took you in my life as a companion firstly and I will always take you back as a companion.

For the Reader

MANSI'S DEATH AFFECTED ME, BUT THIS TIME, I was aware of depression and the only way I could have come out of it was to move on with my life. That's what was needed, that's what she would have wanted, and that's what I did.

The results of the entrance exam were out. I didn't pass the exam. It put me in a position where I was going nowhere in my life, again I left Sitamarhi and went to Kota on 9th April, taking the advice of my family members.

I reached Kota with the motive of preparation; to get selected in Bansal's Acme course. The preparation for that exam kept me motivated for the next two months and eventually I got selected.

The competitive environment of Kota kept me busy and I had little time to think about other things. The new people in the new place with so much of independence kept me 'alive' to rediscover myself again.

You know, there is something majestic about life in Kota. Despite the constant pressure of the performances in the exams, you have to take the responsibility of other things. It gives you a routine life. You are responsible for your food, your clothes, your attitude, and your potential to make friends to support you in the bad times.

It was Kota that gave me another beautiful thing and it was the love of another beautiful girl.

I have been in two good relationships after the death of Mansi. Both the girls were amazing. One of them is Ambika who I have described in the prologue of the novel. Actually it was the break-up with her which brought a lot of questions in my mind.

I am thankful to Shikha for giving me lessons of life. I learned a lot from the relationship with her, and due to that relationship, I was able to bring a lot of changes into my life. The break-up with Shikha gave me the opportunity to recalculate my thoughts on love, life, will power and the future.

Now I can say that there is no such thing like the future. What you have is the present moment. And with my experience of understanding love, life and death, I would suggest to everybody to focus on the present. It's very important to give value to the people who are present around you, because that is the only thing which is true; the future is false.

Every day we lose something whether it is time, money or just a hair. Whatever is the loss, it's painful. Some losses last forever, and each time we recover from it, and with each successive second we hope for something good to happen ... that is how life works.

www.ingramcontent.com/pod-product-compliance
Lightning Source LLC
Chambersburg PA
CBHW051648260626
47170CB00004B/1401